DINING
WITH
ANGELS

DINING WITH ANGELS

Bits & Bites from the Demonica Universe

Short Stories by *New York Times* Bestselling Author
LARISSA IONE

Recipes from *USA Today* Bestselling Author
SUZANNE M. JOHNSON

EVIL EYE
CONCEPTS

Dining With Angels

Copyright 2018 Larissa Ione
Recipes Copyright 2018 Suzanne McCollum Johnson

ISBN: 978-1-948050-63-0

Published by Evil Eye Concepts, Incorporated

All rights reserved. No part of this book may be reproduced, scanned, or distributed in any printed or electronic form without permission. Please do not participate in or encourage piracy of copyrighted materials in violation of the author's rights.

This is a work of fiction. Names, places, characters and incidents are the product of the author's imagination and are fictitious. Any resemblance to actual persons, living or dead, events or establishments is solely coincidental.

A NOTE FROM LARISSA

PART 1

I love food. Love it. In fact, when I travel I plan my itinerary around food and drink. Seriously. I watch shows like Delicious Destinations and keep a file of the restaurants and foods featured in each country and city. Then, along the way during my trip I make sure to stop at these places. I basically eat and drink my way through my vacations. I mean, sightseeing is a vital part of the experience, but give me a Yorkshire pub with locally brewed ale, a Belgian eatery with Flemish Carbonnade, or an Amsterdam restaurant serving poffertjes, and I'm in heaven.

But as much as I love to eat, I'm not a big fan of cooking. My husband actually does most of it. He's a real-life hero, I tell you.

So given the way I glare at the oven, why in the world would I want to publish a cookbook?

Check out the first sentence again: I. Love. Food. And to get good food, it's sometimes necessary to prepare it. And, like most people, I have a day job — sure, as an author I at least get to work in my pajamas — but I simply can't spend a lot of time in the kitchen. If I have to cook, I want to make dishes that are both easy and delicious.

Emphasis on easy.

I have a few trusted, simple, scrumptious recipes I love -- some of which I've included in this book. But really, my talent is geared toward writing fiction, not whipping up homemade mayonnaise.

Lucky for me — and for you — I have an incredible friend who also happens to be a celebrity cook. Confident, genuine, and bursting with Southern charm, Suzanne M. Johnson wields her culinary knowledge like the Grim Reaper wields his scythe. She's utterly fearless in the kitchen! I adore her so much, in fact, that I named a heroine after her, a heroine who is also a fantastic cook with her own cooking show.

I met Suzanne through her sister, Liz Berry, who has become a valued and irreplaceable part of my life, both personally and professionally. The intimate relationship between food, love, and friendship is always on the table when we get together with our buddies (special shout-out to the Beach Babes!) and at author and reader events.

So when Liz suggested that Suzanne and I pair up for a cookbook that would combine my paranormal romance world with Suzanne's culinary expertise, I didn't hesitate. Nothing goes better together than love and food, after all.

Except maybe love and beer. Or vampires and vampire slayers.

So here we are, Suzanne and I, putting our heads and talents together to create pages of tasty recipes and short stories from the Demonica/Lords of Deliverance world that will bring readers up to date on some of their favorite characters' lives. And it makes sense, because food is something that brings everyone together. No matter your race, religion, culture (or species!), everyone eats. Food is something we all have in common. We can learn about each other over a meal (assuming you aren't the meal.) We can expand our palates and our minds by trying new dishes. And we can express ourselves, our individuality, with food.

Are you ready to dive in?

Take my hand, friend, and let's enter this foodie realm together. Your tastebuds will thank you…but your waistline might not!

Love and hugs,

Larissa

A NOTE FROM LARISSA

PART 2

Readers of my Demonica and Lords of Deliverance series know that my books aren't exactly...tame. Like many of the dishes in *this* book, my stories are spicy.

I did, however, want to make *Dining With Angels* a little more family friendly. The problem is that many of my characters are underworld creatures, and demons don't say, "golly gee." They tend to be fond of curse words. So I tricked them. I let them think they could pop off as many F-words as they wanted to, but when they weren't looking, I did a search-and-replace.

Man, they are going to be floofing furious when they see what I did...

TABLE OF CONTENTS

Chapter 1: *Declan and Suzanne* 13

BREAKFAST FOOD/MORNING AFTER 35

    Hair of the Hellhound 36

    Spicy Sheoul Shrimp 37

    Angel Food Cake French Toast 38

    Loaded Grits in a Bacon Cup 39

    Bloody Mary Pie 40

    Pumpkin Spice Loaf with Spiced Icing 42

    Egg in a Hell Hole Avocado Toast 43

    Maple Sausage and Waffle Casserole 44

    Breakfast Burrito 45

Chapter 2: *Wraith and Serena* 47

ROMANTIC/SEXY FOOD 73

    Grilled Oysters with Spicy Butter 74

    Seafood Linguini 75

    Stuffed Flank Steak 76

    Red Devil's Food Cake 77

    Steak Bruschetta with Onion Jam 79

    Bananas Foster Crème Brulee 80

    Caprese Chicken with Balsamic Glaze 81

Chapter 3: *Harvester and Reaver* 83

SPICY FOOD 103

- Dark Chocolate Chipotle Brownies 104
- Grilled Beef Skewers with Wasabi Aioli 105
- White Chicken Chili 106
- Gumbo 107
- Zesty Lemon Mahi Mahi 108
- Salsa with a Vengeance 109
- Spicy Sticky Ribs 110

Chapter 4: *Shade and Runa* 113

FAMILY FRIENDLY FOOD 119

- Hell Frozen Over Smoothie Pops 120
- Meatloaf and Monster Mash Cupcakes 121
- Chicken Parmesan 122
- Cauliflower Pizza 124
- Seafood Platter 125
  - -Fried Shrimp 125
  - -Fried Catfish 126
  - -Buttermilk Hush Hellhound Puppies 126
  - -Beer Battered Fries 127

Chapter 5: *Reseph and Jillian* 129

COMFORT FOOD 148

- Chicken Biscuit Pot Pie 149
- Cherry Hand Pies 150
- Taco Spaghetti 151
- Fried Mac and Cheese Bites 152

French Onion Soup 153

Soft Shell Crab BLT 154

Chapter 6: *Ares and Cara* 155

CELEBRATION FOOD AND SNACKS... 168

Goat Cheese Truffles 169

Seven Layer Greek Goddess 170

Bacon Wrapped Stuffed Figs 171

Mini Chicken Gyros with Easy Tzatziki 172

Pot Stickers 173

Blueberry Lemon Angel Food Cake Trifle 175

Caramel Pretzel Bites...176

Chapter 7: *An Interview with Eidolon and Tayla* 177

WHEN DINING WITH DEMONS... 186

Spaghetti all'Angeliciana 187

Strawberries with Black Pepper Balsamic Sauce 189

RECIPES FROM THE UNDERWORLD... 190

Beer Cheese Spread with Bite...191

Ghastbat (or Chicken) & Cheese Enchiladas
with Green Chili & Sour Cream Sauce.................................... 192

Orecchiette with Hell Weed (or broccoli) and White Beans........... 193

FOR THE HELL PETS 195

Cerby Snacks 195

Hellcat Bits 196

Hellhound Bites 197

Paw Balm 198

A bagel is a doughnut with the sin removed.
~George Rosenbaum

DECLAN and SUZANNE

Hair of the Hellhound

Spicy Sheoul Shrimp

Angel Food Cake French Toast

Loaded Grits in a Bacon Cup

Bloody Mary Pie

Pumpkin Spice Loaf with Spiced Icing

Egg in a Hell Hole Avocado Toast

Maple Sausage and Waffle Casserole

Breakfast Burrito

DECLAN AND SUZANNE

Suzanne Burke smiled into the camera and held up a fork laden with a bite of her special Bloody Mary Pie.

"And that is how you make a savory morning-after brunch your mate will never forget. Perfectly paired with a shot of cucumber-infused vodka or a zesty Hair of the Hellhound." She took a bite and nearly moaned in ecstasy. She loved this dish, and happily, it was also one of Declan's favorites. "Mmm. Spicy, tangy, and decadent. See you next time, when my special guests will be two real life angels. And remember, you can see all my past episodes and recipes on my YouTube channel. Just click the menu button to find the perfect dish for any occasion, whether you're dining with angels, drinking with demons, or hanging with humans." She gave an air-toast with the shot of vodka placed next to the pie. "Until next time, my friends. Blessings to all."

"Cut!"

Suzanne breathed a sigh of relief as taping for her cable network cooking show, Angel in the Kitchen, ended.

"That was your best episode to date." Kimberly, Suzanne's producer, gave her a thumbs up and handed her a stack of messages. "Most of these have been handled, including the request from your cookbook editor for an updated file for one of your recipes, but you're going to want to address the top one yourself. It's a message from your stepmom. She thought she dialed your cell phone but got the show line instead. Said it must be pregnancy brain. She was hoping you had a recipe for late-term morning sickness."

Suzanne's stepmother, Lilliana, had been staying with Ares, first Horseman of the Apocalypse, and his wife, Cara, who was well into her third trimester of pregnancy and, according to Lilliana, she'd had a rough time of it. Odd, though, that Lilliana had claimed pregnancy brain, given that it was Cara who was pregnant. But then, Lilliana had been helping Cara for months — maybe she had sympathy brain.

"Thanks, Kim." Suzanne reached up and released her wavy brown hair from the ponytail she'd put it in while she'd cooked. "I'll call her back when I get home."

Kim checked her watch. "Which, if you get moving, could be as soon as a few seconds."

"Nah. I'm going to flash to Dallas to see Declan first."

Belatedly she glanced around to make sure none of the human show crew were listening. Kim, a werewolf since she was bitten fifteen years ago, had tried to ensure that as many of their crew as possible were underworlders, but for various reasons, about half the crew were human, and only a handful of those were "in the know." And because Suzanne's father was controlling and paranoid, he'd insisted that she hire one of her siblings as her assistant-slash-bodyguard, as if Suzanne's angelic powers weren't enough to protect her.

Plus she had Declan, and while he was, technically, human, he'd been... upgraded. Anyone trying to get to her would have to go through him and vice versa.

"What's he doing in Dallas?" Kim asked.

"It's where he works."

Kim's brown eyes rolled behind her funky red horn-rimmed glasses. "Yes, I know that. You flash him back and forth to work with DART. But wasn't he recently in Dallas to visit friends from his former job?"

Declan had worked as a bodyguard for the Dallas-based McKay-Taggart office after serving in the military, and he kept in contact with many of his old buddies. Sometimes McKay-Taggart's big boss, Ian, even consulted with Declan on some of their stranger cases, since Dec had earned a reputation of being the guy to call when shit got weird.

"He needs to hang out with humans who don't know the truth about us sometimes," Suzanne said. "Between my family and his job with the Demonic Activity Response Team, I think he gets overwhelmed by immortals and underworlders."

"I get that," Kim sighed. "It took me a while to adjust."

Suzanne completely understood. She herself had grown up believing she was human, and it had been a huge shock to learn she was Memitim, a class of earthbound angel bred to be a guardian of beings important to the fate of humanity. She no longer served in that capacity, but she was still in service to the forces of good.

"How'd you finally do it?" she asked. "Adjust, I mean."

Kim shuffled the papers in her hands as she spoke. She was never idle. "I got new friends."

"You dumped all your human friends?"

"Pretty much." Kim nudged her glasses higher up her nose. "It's too hard to lie, and it got to the point where I couldn't talk about my problems with them because I couldn't tell them the truth, you know?" She gave a wan smile. "It all worked out in the end. I miss my family, though."

"You dumped your family too?"

"Oh, no. I went werewolf one night and ate them all." When Suzanne gasped in horror, Kim laughed. "I'm kidding. Honey, you are so gullible. My family is alive and well and living in Connecticut. I see them all the time. Which, frankly, is too much."

Now, *that*, Suzanne definitely got. She loved her angelic family, but she had literally thousands of fellow Memitim siblings, several of whom hung out at her New York apartment, and her father was the Grim Reaper. Her family could definitely be…intense, and she didn't blame Declan for needing a break now and then.

Angel in the Kitchen's assistant producer, Phillippa, waved to Kim, and she gave a "be right there," gesture before turning back to Suzanne. "I'll have some clips for you to approve later tonight. See you at the next prep meeting."

Suzanne grabbed her stuffed-to-capacity tote bag and looped the handles over her shoulder. "Sounds good. See you tomorrow."

Pulse pounding in anticipation of seeing Declan, she headed to her office, where she could safely dematerialize without anyone seeing. As she walked down the halls, past studio execs, crews from other shows, and even a couple of actors dressed in alien costumes, she marveled at how her life had turned out.

She was married to the man of her dreams, she had a top-rated cooking show on a science fiction network, and her food was a "culinary marvel," according to top critics who couldn't explain why her dishes left people feeling exactly the way she said they would, whether it was happy, content, aroused, or energetic. They didn't know that her angelic powers infused her recipes, nor were they aware that her show was a hit among underworlders who knew that the show's premise of her being an angel who catered to vampires, demons, werewolves, *and* humans wasn't fiction.

There were so many ways she was blessed, and she couldn't imagine anything better.

Well, she could.

But she didn't see Declan giving up the dangers of his job anytime soon.

"Declan!" Kynan Morgan shouted, his already deep voice, raspy from vocal cord damage taken during his military days, going even lower with urgency. "Kill it! Kill the damned demon now!"

Declan shot his colleague a glare as he pivoted on the blood-slippery floor of the burned out factory and raised his gore-covered hatchet. "What the hell do you think I'm trying to do?"

The demon, an ivory-skinned monster covered in oozing red spines, was swelling up like a puffer fish, and it was only a matter of seconds before it launched those poisonous spines like arrows at every one of the DART crew members fighting the nest of demons in the abandoned building.

Feinting left, Declan barely avoided being eviscerated by the demon's six-inch razor-sharp claws. His swing with the hatchet went wild, catching the beast at the base of its thorny tail instead of in its bare underbelly. Quickly, before the demon blew its spines, he activated the set of enchanted wings tattooed on his back. The swath of skin between his shoulder blades tingled as massive, nearly transparent wings shot skyward and lifted him into the air. The demon screamed in fury, leaping to catch him, but Declan went into a spinning dive, closing the distance between them in a heartbeat.

With a shout of victory, he slammed the hatchet home, burying the blade between the beast's crimson eyes.

Yes!

"Dec! Watch out!"

He didn't have time to react. Something crunched into his face and knocked him out of the air. Pain exploded in his head and the world became a blur as he tumbled across the ground and slammed into a support pillar.

"Shit!" Tayla's shout pierced the ringing in Declan's ears, and then she was kneeling next to him as he lay sprawled on the ground. "Hold still, buddy. We'll get a healer to you."

"**Alfargchgarayte.**" He groaned, unsure what he'd said or even what he'd meant to say. Clearly, his jaw was broken, and if the throbbing agony in his cheek and skull was any indication, there were a lot of shattered bones in his head.

He heard voices all around, some pained, some freaking out a little. This had been a big battle, the biggest one he'd been involved with since he'd learned the truth about the existence of demons. As a member of the secret, government-sanctioned Demonic Activity Response Team, he'd been investigating non-friendly underworld incursions into the human realm and had engaged in a lot of minor fights and skirmishes, but this one had taken the entire team by surprise. Good thing Kynan and Tayla, the big bosses who usually worked the Eastern Seaboard, had chosen today to accompany the Dallas unit on an investigation.

"Declan?" His supervisor's voice drifted down to him. "**Dec?**" Corey's face hovered above his, her normally spiky blonde hair plastered against her skull by blood. Demon blood, he hoped. She tapped his shoulder. "Stay with us, Dec. Stay with us..."

Her voice faded, and he welcomed the silence almost as much as he welcomed the pain-free blackness that swallowed him. His last thought before he lost consciousness was that Suzanne was never going to let this go...

"Don't worry," Kynan said. "It's not as bad as it sounds."

Suzanne's heart leaped into her throat as she stood in the living room of the apartment she and Declan maintained in Dallas. It had been Dec's bachelor pad when he was single, and they'd kept it as a cover so his human friends wouldn't know he was actually commuting from New York via Suzanne's angelic taxi service, as he called it.

Now the apartment was packed with Declan's colleagues at DART. Colleagues covered in blood and bandages. Everyone except Kynan, anyway. Suzanne didn't know the whole story, but he'd apparently been charmed by angels and gifted with some sort of immunity to injury by demons. She'd have to ask him about it someday.

Someday after she forgave him for allowing Declan to be hurt.

She grabbed him by the arm. "What do you mean it's not as bad as it sounds? Where is he?"

"He's in the bedroom, but—"

She didn't wait for Kynan to finish. She sprinted into the bedroom to find Declan, clad in only a pair of sweatpants, sitting on the bed with an icepack at his temple. A male in hospital scrubs stood in front of him, one hand on Declan's shoulder. The glyphs that spanned the entire length of the doctor's fingers, hand, and arm glowed with power that cut off as the door closed behind her.

Declan looked over at her with a smile. "Hey. Good timing. Eidolon is just finishing."

Weird. She hadn't known that the infamous demon doctor who ran Underworld General Hospital made house calls. When she thought about it, though, it made sense, given that he was mated to Tayla, who had been in the living room when Suzanne arrived.

Suzanne nodded in greeting, hoping her wariness didn't show. Most demons lived in Sheoul, a hell realm run by a fallen angel named Revenant after a coup that ended with Satan imprisoned, but some, like Eidolon and his siblings, lived among unsuspecting humans. And just like humans, demons came in all shades of good and evil, a yin-yang effect that balanced out the universe. Eidolon was considered one of the rare good demons. An ally, even.

But even though she'd worked with Eidolon's brother Wraith and she herself had once been treated at UG, the demon still made her nervous, as if she should keep her defensive powers on tap in case she needed to use them quickly.

"What happened?" She moved to Declan and sank down on the mattress beside him as Eidolon tucked his stethoscope into his medical bag. Declan looked tired, and fading bruises marred the left side of his face and jaw, but his smile was bright.

"I got nailed by a Noirmal demon. Bastards ambushed us."

"Dammit, Declan," she murmured. "You could have been killed."

He put down the icepack and took her hand in his. It was cold from the ice, and all she could think about was that his hand would feel the same if he was dead.

"I'm immortal," he reminded her. "I was perfectly safe."

"Immortal doesn't mean invincible. There are things not even immortals can survive."

Eidolon hefted the bag over his shoulder. "She's right," he said, and she decided she liked this demon doctor. "I've seen a lot of immortals become really floofing mortal when their heads are chopped off or their hearts are ripped out of their chests."

"See?" She gestured to the demon. "You should listen to your doctor."

"I was perfectly fine," Declan insisted. "Journey didn't show up, so obviously I was in no real danger."

Journey, one of her thousands of brothers, had been appointed as Declan's guardian angel after she'd been reassigned, and as Dec's protector, he'd have been alerted if Declan had been in a life-threatening situation.

But that still didn't make her feel any better. She didn't like seeing Declan hurt, and the thought of losing him sent her into a cold panic.

"I don't think you should work for DART anymore."

Declan laughed, but when she stared at him, his steel gray eyes shot wide. "What, you're serious?"

"I don't want to lose you." She shifted so she was facing him. "Watching what my father is going through with Lilliana is horrible. I know their separation is only temporary, but he aches for her. I don't want to go through that with you."

Declan brought her hand to his lips and pressed a tender, reassuring kiss into her palm. "You won't go through that. I'm careful. And you know this is something I have to do."

Yes, she did. Declan had a deep, instinctive need to help people, a duty to mankind he couldn't shake...nor would he want to. But that didn't mean he had to expose himself to danger on a daily basis.

"You could help mankind in safer ways, you know. You were a medic." She glanced over at Eidolon. "You could work in a hospital or something."

The doctor held up his hands. "Hey, don't look at me. I offered him a job."

She gaped at Declan. "And you refused?"

Eidolon moved toward the door, his shoes not making a sound even on the floorboards that normally squeaked. "So, I'm just going to go where I'm not in the middle of a married couple's spat." He reached for the doorknob. "Dec, I healed most of the damage, but some of the bruising will have to go away on its own. Aspirin should help the residual aches and pains. Call if there are any complications or you have any questions." He gave a sheepish grin. "And the job offer still stands."

"Thank you, doctor," she said. "He'll think about it."

"No, he won't," Declan called out as Eidolon slipped into the hallway.

Suzanne couldn't help but smile and shake her head. He was stubborn, but she loved him for it. "You know I'll keep bugging you to change jobs."

He tossed the icepack aside and stretched out on the mattress, propping himself up on one elbow. The waistband of his sweats had fallen low on his hips, revealing hard-cut abs and a shadowy hint of skin in the hollow of his pelvis that she suddenly wanted to lave with her tongue.

"I wouldn't expect anything else from you." His voice was low, husky, and full of erotic undertones.

Damn him, he could distract her so easily, and no doubt he was doing it intentionally. "I know you need to do what you love," she sighed, "but I still worry about you."

He waggled his blond brows. "I *do* do what I love." He patted the mattress next to him, the muscles in his thick arms rippling. "Come here and I'll do you right now."

"Just a sec." Unable to withstand his charm, she hurried to the door and opened it just enough to shout through the crack. "Hey, everyone, thanks for everything, but I'll take it from here."

There was a chorus of "see you laters," and "feel better soons," and then the front door closed and everything went quiet.

When she turned back around, the X-rated promise swirling in Declan's eyes made her breath catch. "Don't move," he said in a dark, seductive voice. "Just let me look at you."

"Wanna see more of me?" she teased as she peeled off her blouse. "I mean, as long as you feel up to it."

"Oh," he growled softly, "I'm up to it."

A glance at the tent in his sweats offered proof of his words, and warmth spread through every one of her erogenous zones. With slow, deliberate motions, she kicked off her heels and unbuttoned her pants, enjoying the way his predatory gaze watched every move she made. When she was left in nothing but her matching teal and black lace panties and bra, she walked over to him, anticipation making her heart pound in an erratic rhythm.

As she approached, he rolled onto his back and made a "come on" gesture with his fingers. "Seeing how I'm injured, I should probably just lay here."

Smiling seductively, she climbed onto the bed and straddled his thighs, giving him a prime view of her cleavage. "So you want me to do all the work?"

He reached up and cupped a breast through the fabric, and she had to bite back a moan as his thumb flicked over a nipple. "Is it really…work?"

"Mmm." She arched into his touch. "Not when you do that."

Suddenly, the hair on the back of her neck tingled, and light flashed in her peripheral vision.

"Oh, shit!" a male voice shouted. "My eyes! My eyes!"

Declan and Suzanne jumped simultaneously, and she let out a startled yelp as her brother -- Declan's guardian angel -- Journey, stood in the middle of the bedroom, his hands plastered over his face.

This was just not her day.

Declan shot off the mattress and scrambled to cover Suzanne with the nearest object, which happened to be a pillow.

"Dude!" he shouted as he tugged up his sweatpants. "What the hell? We established rules when I agreed to join this insane family, and **not** popping into our homes unannounced, especially our *bedrooms*, is one of them." He swept Suzanne's clothes off the floor and tossed them to her. "I know you're ancient as floof, but we have these things called phones now."

"And doorbells," Suzanne chimed in as she shoved her feet into her pants.

"Yeah..." Journey rubbed the back of his neck, gaze cast downward, his dark, shaggy hair concealing his expression. "Trust me, I'm more traumatized than you are. Ugh. It's like that time someone sent me a link and I was dumb enough to click on it. It was floofing **sock puppet** porn." He shuddered. "Did you know that existed? There's not enough eye bleach in the world."

Hopped up on adrenaline and unquenched lust, Declan barely kept his patience in check. "Why. Are. You. Here."

Journey, who seemed to avoid being serious at all costs, grew quiet, his expression grim. Which tripped Declan's *oh, shit* alarm. "It's Azagoth."

Suzanne shimmied into her top. "What's our father done now?"

"He's closed Sheoul-gra. No one can get in or out. Not even *griminions*."

Declan had never been to the Grim Reaper's realm, which was a holding tank for the souls of demons and evil humans, but closing it sounded like it might be a big deal.

"What?" Suzanne froze as she reached for her shoes. "That's...that's unprecedented. And bad. Really bad."

"*Griminions*," Declan mused. "They're your father's creepy little soul-collectors, right?"

Suzanne nodded. "They gather thousands of souls a day. If the *griminions* aren't able to deliver the souls to Sheoul-gra, they'll be loose, free to cause chaos in the demon and human realms." She pivoted back to Journey. "Why did he do it? How do you know about this? Are communications still up?"

Journey toyed with the plug in his earlobe. "Comms are shut down too. He warned us seconds before he did it. I got out to let everyone know what was going on."

"But why? Why did he do it? Does it have something to do with Lilliana?"

"I don't know," Journey said, "but our father is in a rage like I've never seen before -- and I've seen him rage-morph into a dragon-demon and literally explode like a bomb. We need to do something, and we need to do it fast."

Declan swiped his cell phone off the end table. "I can call DART. Maybe they'll have some insight into what's going on."

"I have a better idea," Suzanne said. "There's only one person who can deal with Azagoth when he's on a Reaper rampage."

Journey cocked a pierced eyebrow. "You mean Lilliana? Good luck. I tried to see her a couple of weeks back. Apparently, she wasn't 'feeling well.'"

Declan remembered Suzanne saying the same thing when she'd tried to visit her stepmother recently. Whatever was going on between Azagoth and Lilliana was very, very private.

"Well," Suzanne said, her brown eyes sparking with the stubborn fire Declan loved -- when it wasn't aimed at him—"I happen to know the very thing that will make her feel better."

"Lemme guess," Journey said. "Food?"

She patted his cheek as she brushed past him on her way to the door. "See, that's why everyone says you're the smart brother."

Journey beamed. "They do?"

Declan rolled his eyes and gave his brother-in-law a comforting clap on the back. "Sure, man. Sure."

Dec joined Suzanne, laughing as Journey called out after them, "You two are assholes, you know that?"

As if Declan hadn't heard that before. Silly angel.

Suzanne grabbed the tote bag she'd left in the living room. "I'm going to whip up something to take to Cara. Do you want to go with me or stay here?"

He took her hand so she could flash him with her. "I'm with you, sweetheart. Always."

Her smile was blinding, and it almost made up for the fact that her idiot brother had interrupted what he was sure would have been a marathon session between the sheets.

But that was the thing about being immortal; if one didn't get his or her head chopped off, eternity was made of marathons.

Suzanne spent a couple of hours preparing her favorite comfort food, Mac and Cheese Bites, for Lilliana, as well as a few snack samples for Cara's baby shower, and then she and Declan flashed to Ares's Greek island. They materialized inside the designated landing spot among the olive trees near the massive mansion just as the sun was setting, its golden rays glinting off the white sand and the sea beyond the beach.

The secret island, hidden from human eyes thanks to some sort of magic, was a paradise no one could access without permission, which she'd secured with a quick call to Cara.

Cara, wearing an elegant aqua maternity gown with matching sandals, met them at the front door. Suzanne had only met the very pregnant hellhound whisperer once when she'd come to help plan Cara's baby shower menu, but Cara greeted her like an old friend.

"It's so good to see you again," Cara said as she engulfed Suzanne in a hug. "But I'm afraid you came for nothing. Lilliana isn't feeling well and doesn't want to see anyone."

"It's really important. Did you tell her that?"

"I did."

Suzanne cursed softly, and Declan laughed. He didn't consider "crap" to be a curse word.

"Will you please try again? It's about Azagoth. It's rather urgent." She handed Cara the container of food samples. "These are some of the dishes we discussed the other day. I figured that since I was going to be here, I might as well bring them for you to try."

"How thoughtful." Cara smiled as she gave the container a sniff. "Come on in. I'll give it another shot with Lilliana, but don't get your hopes up."

Declan and Suzanne entered the palatial estate, their shoes clicking on the marble floor. Cara left them in the main living room, where Declan went taut at the sight of the huge man-goat demons clomping around, one with a dust mop and another with a tray of iced tea.

"It's okay," she whispered to Declan. "They're servants, totally loyal to Ares and Cara."

"This is so floofed up." He gave her a pointed look. "See, **that's** how you curse. With conviction and crassness." He sucked in a harsh breath as a hellhound as tall as a draft horse and twice as long padded across the room, its crimson eyes measuring them for meals before it disappeared down a hallway. "I'm never going to get used to this," he muttered, adding another crass curse with conviction.

He kept cursing as they wandered around admiring the ancient Greek and Roman artifacts Ares had collected over the eons until Cara returned a couple of minutes later.

"I'm shocked," she said, "but Lilliana gave permission. Her suite is down the corridor and to the right. It's the double doors at the end of the hall."

Remaining box of food in hand, Suzanne and Declan hurried to Lilliana's suite. She tapped on the door and heard a shouted, "Come in! I'm on the balcony."

They entered into a luxurious room decorated with Greek art and furniture. Black and gold pottery dotted the shelves, and a life-sized marble horse took up a corner near the dining set that could comfortably seat twelve.

"Wow." Declan's eyes shot wide. "And I thought our place in New York was big."

"The Horsemen are larger than life," she said. "And they do everything to scale."

They walked past the kitchen and saw Lilliana through the open sliding glass doors, her back to them as she stood at the balcony railing overlooking the sea. Her long chestnut hair was loose and blowing around her shoulders, which were bare except for the delicate straps on her gauzy orange top. White harem pants and bare feet completed the outfit that seemed perfect for hanging out in a Greek paradise.

But was it really paradise when you weren't with your loved one? When you were standing by yourself on a balcony made for romance?

Suzanne hadn't seen her stepmom, an angel of a different Order who had originally been sent to Azagoth as Heaven's version of a mail-order bride, in months, not since she'd left Azagoth. Suzanne didn't know exactly why she'd left, but she'd bet her wings that it was her father's fault. She loved him, but the Grim Reaper could be a serious jerk.

"Thanks for seeing us," she began. "I'm sorry you aren't feeling well."

"I'm feeling fine," Lilliana said, still facing the water.

"Then why--" She broke off as the other woman turned around, revealing a very swollen, very pregnant belly. *Holy shit.* "Oh. Oh...wow."

Lilliana smiled and rubbed her baby bump. "No one knows except Ares, Cara, Reaver, and Harvester, and I'd like to keep it that way."

"But my father knows." **Please, please say he knows.** "Right?"

Lilliana shook her head and Suzanne's gut dropped to her feet. Lilliana must have a good reason for keeping this huge secret, but...Azagoth didn't have a reputation of being very forgiving when he felt he was wronged. He was going to flip out. A lot.

"You said you're here because of Azagoth?" Lilliana took a sip of the orange juice balanced on the railing next to her, and Suzanne swore she saw Lilliana's hand shake.

"Yes. He just shut down Sheoul-gra. No one can get in or out. We were hoping you might know why."

Lilliana blew out a relieved breath and sagged against the deck railing, nearly spilling her juice. "So it's not just me."

"What do you mean?" Concern laced Declan's voice as he moved closer to Lilliana, his body taut, as if he was preparing to catch her if she went down.

"I tried to go home today, but I couldn't get in." She glanced up at a sea bird riding the wind overhead, and when she looked back at Suzanne, her gaze was a little brighter. "I thought maybe Azagoth had locked me out. I didn't know why he would, though. We Skyped just last night and everything was great. So great that it cemented my decision to go this morning."

Declan frowned. "He has a temper, right?"

Lilliana snorted. "A temper. How cute."

"Well, what if he learned you were pregnant?" Declan asked. "Would that have made him lose his shit?"

"Definitely." Lilliana put down her juice. "But I don't know how he'd have found out. I've been sequestered on Ares's island since I left Sheoul-gra."

Azagoth had spies everywhere, but Ares ran a tight ship and only a fool would betray the Horseman known as War. "Do you know any other reason why he might have done it?" Suzanne asked.

"It had to have been something big," Lilliana said, her brow furrowed in thought. "He knows what kind of damage demon and evil souls can do if they aren't taken to Sheoul-gra immediately. And he certainly wouldn't prevent Memitim from leaving to do their jobs. It makes no sense." She brushed past Declan and Suzanne on her way inside. "Let me see if I can contact him."

They waited on the balcony while she tried to contact Azagoth, and when she returned, the worry in her expression told them she'd failed.

"I tried calling, Skyping, emailing, and texting," she said. "Nothing."

"I figured as much," Suzanne sighed. "Journey said comms were down." She realized she was still holding the container of Mac and Cheese Bites she'd brought for Lilliana, and she held them out. "These are for you. Specially infused with love and comforting vibes."

"Oh, Suzanne," Lilliana murmured as she took the food. "I've always adored you. Thank you."

The feeling was mutual. In fact, most of Suzanne's brothers and sisters loved Lilliana. There were a few who treated her like an evil stepmother, but for the most part, everyone recognized that if not for Lilliana, their father would be a very different, very horrible, person.

Declan's phone beeped softly, barely audible over the crashing of the waves on the rocks below. "It's Hawkyn," he said, looking down at the screen. "He's at our apartment. He might have news. We'd better go."

Hopefully her brother and mentor, who had recently been given the role of liaison between Heaven and Sheoul-gra, would know something. Suzanne turned back to Lilliana. "If you hear anything...anything at all, call me."

"You do the same." Lilliana gestured to her belly. "And not a word to anyone. Not even Hawkyn, and especially not Azagoth." She reached out and took Suzanne's hand. "I know it's not in you to lie or keep things from your brother. But it's only for a little while. It's time for me to go back to Sheoul-gra. As soon as it's open, and as soon as I know it's safe, I'll go."

Suzanne agreed, but she hoped Sheoul-gra would open soon, because Lilliana didn't look like she had much time to spare before giving birth. And Suzanne couldn't even begin to imagine how furious Azagoth would be if he didn't get to be present for the birth of his child.

Because although Azagoth had thousands of children, he hadn't been there for a single birth, and to be denied the one he should have been part of...

She shuddered. If ever there was a time to move Heaven and Earth for something, this was it.

Hawkyn and another of Suzanne's closest brothers, Maddox, were waiting for them when she and Declan materialized in the living room. Mad was in the middle of downing a beer, while Hawk was doing something on his phone.

"It's about time," Hawk said, looking up from the screen. "Where were you?"

"It's been two seconds since Declan got your message." Stomach suddenly growling, Suzanne headed for the kitchen, hoping her brothers hadn't eaten the leftovers from dinner last night. "And we were checking in on Lilliana."

Mad put down his beer bottle on the kitchen island with a heavy clank. "Seriously? You were actually able to talk to her? To see her? She's refused visits from everyone."

"Yeah," Dec said, "we saw her. Figured it couldn't hurt to see if she knew anything about why Azagoth shut down Sheoul-gra."

Hawkyn blew out a long, ragged breath, and Suzanne froze with her hand on the fridge door handle. This wasn't going to be good. "What is it?" she asked, slowly turning to her brother.

"He flipped out," Maddox said, his voice grave. "Went supernova." Swallowing hard, he closed his eyes. "I don't blame him."

Hawkyn jammed his hand through his blond hair, leaving messy spikes behind. "A new batch of our brothers and sisters arrived last week. Teens. Total pains in the asses."

Despite his harsh words, Hawk smiled fondly. He'd taken a number of new arrivals under his wings. All adult Memitim had. The kids had been raised according to the rules, among humans, clueless as to their real origins and species, and now they were living in Sheoul-gra, training to be guardian angels someday. For most, the transition had been easy, but some still resisted, and Hawk had volunteered to mentor the most difficult of them.

"Okay," Dec said. "So what's the big deal?"

"One of them was murdered," Hawkyn blurted, and Suzanne gasped.

"Inside Sheoul-gra?" At Maddox's nod, Suzanne sank numbly down on a bar stool. "What happened?"

"I don't know." Hawkyn's emerald eyes, so like their father's, flashed with anger. "I was looking into a lead about Cipher when Azagoth summoned me. He let me inside Sheoul-gra, but I'm the only one he's unlocked the gates for."

"And he's only letting people out after he's interrogated them," Maddox added. "It wasn't...pleasant."

Suzanne could only imagine. She glanced over at Hawkyn, who still seemed shaken. "What happened when he summoned you?"

"He demanded that I track down everyone who had been in or out of Sheoul-gra in the twenty-four hours before and after the murder. He's got Hades checking to make sure no one traveled to or from the Inner Sanctum."

The Inner Sanctum was the true hell that humans often talked about when they referred to Hell. Consisting of progressively horrific levels, or "rings," it was where the evil and demon souls were kept until they were reincarnated and sent back to the demon realm, Sheoul. Hades, a fallen angel with a Mohawk and the fun-loving personality of a drunk cobra, ran the Inner Sanctum, and no one got in or out without his knowledge.

"It's not going to be long before evil souls start piling up if *griminions* can't deliver them," Mad said. "I've already heard from some of our siblings that the evil spirits are attacking humans. We have to get Azagoth to open the gates."

Hawkyn snorted. "Once our father has made a decision, nothing can change it."

"There's always Lilliana," Declan said.

Maddox tossed a pillow from the couch at Declan. "She left him, dumbass. Or did you forget?"

"She wants to go home." Suzanne idly pulled her iPad toward her, as if the recipes she stored on it could help somehow. Unfortunately, she didn't know of any dishes that could knock some sense into the Grim Reaper. Well, maybe an *actual* dish. A really heavy one, like an iron skillet. "In fact, she tried this morning but couldn't get in."

Hawkyn's tawny eyebrows rose. "Really? That...that might be the answer. Can she contact him?"

"She tried," Declan said, "but no luck. Comms are still down."

"Wait." Suzanne rolled her lower lip between her teeth as a plan started to form. "Our father might not allow incoming communications, but he wouldn't shut down *his* ability to communicate with the outside world. I think I can get through to him."

"How?" Declan, Hawkyn, and Maddox asked simultaneously.

"He gets alerts when I post new episodes of Angel in the Kitchen." She grinned as she turned on her iPad. "I think it's time for an online special."

Declan had grown up in the sleazy world of wealth and politics. It had shaped his views on life, marriage, and his career. He'd been uncompromising. Self-destructive. A total asshole as well.

But then Suzanne had come along. He hadn't known she was an angel at the time. Hadn't known he was a special person called a Primori, a being fated to play an important role in the future of the planet. Nor had he known that she was his angelic bodyguard. Heck, he'd believed that *he* was *her* bodyguard.

It had been a real punch to the head when he'd learned the truth.

Angels were real. Demons, vampires, and werewolves were real. And he was lucky enough to have been welcomed into that very real world.

It hit home as he watched Suzanne tape a web-exclusive episode of Angel in the Kitchen that would be seen by thousands but that was meant for an audience of one.

She loved her family and her life, but she'd seen a lot of tragedy and was willing to do absolutely anything to prevent suffering. Right now she was focused on the suffering of her father and stepmother, but earlier in the day she'd been worried about *his* suffering. She'd brought Declan into her close circle and had given him, literally, a higher purpose. He'd never felt as though he could pay her back, but he suddenly knew how.

While she prepared her food and spoke to the camera as if she were speaking to a room of good friends, he made a call.

He got off the phone just in time to watch her wrap things up.

"See?" she said as she held up a plate of Angel Food Cake French Toast. "Easy to make, but everyone will think you spent hours on it. It's a dish my father, the Grim Reaper, loves. And Father, if you're watching, you should know that I spoke to Lilliana today, and she'd very much like to make this for you herself, as soon as possible. You just have to open your heart."

By "heart," she meant "gate," but there was no reason to let Azagoth's many enemies know that Sheoul-gra was experiencing some...technical difficulties.

Declan watched Suz wrap things up, and when everything was finished, he kicked Maddox and Hawkyn out of the apartment. She normally did tapings from the TV studio, but the network had given her leeway to make short web exclusives from home whenever she wanted to.

"Well," she said as she let down her hair. "Do you think that'll work?"

"Let's hope so. While you were taping I spoke to one of my DART supervisors, Scott, and he said that demonic incursions were on the rise. He suspects that the demon souls that should be in Sheoul-gra are causing the issues." He took her hand and pulled her down on the couch beside him. "And I spoke to him about something else."

She narrowed her gorgeous eyes at him. "This sounds serious."

Tugging her closer, he brushed a lock of wavy hair from her face and tucked it behind her ear. "I love you. And I love my job."

She went taut. "Is this about what I said earlier? About quitting DART? Because I didn't mean it. I was just afraid and overreacting."

"It is about that," he admitted. "But I understand. I mean, you're a badass, tough-as-floof angel, and I still worry about you. I was so floofing relieved when you were taken off bodyguard duty and allowed to host a cooking show."

She inhaled, holding her breath for a tense moment before blurting, "What...what are you trying to say?"

"I'm saying that you were right." Man, it hurt to admit that, but as his old Air Force supervisor once told him, "When you're wrong, admit it. Don't be wrong *and* a dick." His words might not have been worthy of a meme or anything, but they were true.

"I can't change who I am," Declan continued, "but I can make it better for you. I didn't quit DART, but I quit the Dallas team. I'm transferring to the New York division. I know distance isn't an issue for you since you can flash anywhere you want, but it's an issue for me. Plus, I'll be working with Kynan and Tayla, two of the most experienced demon slayers on the planet."

He'd figured Suzanne would be pleased with his news, but he wasn't expecting the way her eyes filled with tears as she threw herself into his arms.

"You didn't have to do that," she said against his neck. "But I'm so glad you did."

He was too. There was nothing more important than family, and now that he had an amazing one, he wasn't going to do anything to screw it up. At least, not today.

Tomorrow might be another story, but as long as he had Suzanne, he knew, without a doubt, that there would always be a happy ending.

I hope you enjoyed this peek into the married lives of Declan and Suzanne! If you'd like to read more about them, you can find their story between the pages of Her Guardian Angel. Or, if you want to meet them before they find their happily-ever-after, check out Lexi Blake's Close Cover for a little about Declan, or my own HAWKYN, where Suzanne finds her footing. Happy reading!

BREAKFAST/MORNING AFTER FOOD

Hair of the Hellhound

2 tablespoons Cajun seasoning

16 ounces tomato juice

4 ounces vodka

2 tablespoons lemon juice

1 tablespoon pickle juice

¼ teaspoon celery salt

¼ teaspoon pepper

1 tablespoon Worcestershire sauce

¼ teaspoon horseradish

1 teaspoon hot sauce

Wet the rim of two pint glasses then dip each glass into the Cajun seasoning. Fill the glasses halfway with ice. In a large pitcher, mix together all remaining ingredients. Pour mixture into the prepared glasses and garnish with your choice of toppings.

Garnish ideas:

Spicy Sheoul Shrimp

Sliced bacon

Baby dill pickles

Cherry tomatoes

Green olives

Angel feathers

Fairy wings

Sprinkle of Angel Dust

Spicy Sheoul Shrimp

8 cups water

1 cup Cajun seasoning

1 pound (16-24 count) shrimp, peeled and deveined

In a large pot, bring water to a full boil with 1 tablespoon of the Cajun seasoning. Add the shrimp and boil until pink, about 2-3 minutes. Drain shrimp and add immediately to a large bowl of ice water. Allow the shrimp to cool in the ice water for 2-3 minutes. Drain on paper towels then dredge each shrimp into the remaining Cajun seasoning.

Angel Food Cake French Toast

3 large eggs

1 cup milk

1 teaspoon vanilla extract

1 teaspoon ground nutmeg

1 angel food cake, sliced into 12 pieces

3 tablespoons butter

Black and Blue Syrup

1 teaspoon cinnamon

Whipped cream

In a large bowl, whisk together eggs, milk, vanilla extract, ground nutmeg and cinnamon. Heat a large skillet over medium heat. Gently dip each piece of angel food cake into the egg mixture, fully submerging it and covering all sides. Make sure to let most of the egg drip off. Place ½ tablespoon of butter into the skillet and add 2-3 slices of cake. Cook until golden brown on each side, about 2-3 minutes per side. Repeat with remaining slices. Top with Black and Blue Syrup and whipped cream.

Black and Blue Syrup

1 cup fresh blueberries

1 cup fresh blackberries

¾ cup sugar

½ cup water

Place blueberries and blackberries in a food processor and pulse 2-3 times until most of the berries are chopped. Do not completely puree. In a small pot, add the berries, sugar and water and bring to a boil. Reduce heat and simmer for 20 minutes. Place in a pourable container and serve.

Loaded Grits in a Bacon Cup

12 strips bacon (6 whole strips, 6 cut in half)

6 cups water

1 tablespoon salt

2 cups milk

4 cups instant grits

8 tablespoons (1 stick) butter

1 (8 ounce) package cream cheese

2 cups mozzarella cheese

2 cups sharp cheddar cheese

1 teaspoon pepper

¼ cup green onion

Preheat oven to 400 degrees. Using a 6-cup muffin tin, turn the tin upside down and place 2 half-strips of bacon on top, making an X. Then place 1 whole strip of bacon around the sides to form a cup. Repeat with remaining bacon strips. Place muffin tin on a rimmed cookie sheet. Bake for 20 minutes, remove bacon cups from cupcake tin and drain on paper towels. While the bacon cups are baking, prepare the loaded grits. In a large pot, bring water and salt to a roaring boil. Add milk and grits and stir continuously until they begin to thicken. Cover pot and turn to low. Allow to cook for about 5-10 minutes, then remove from heat and add butter and cream cheese. When they have been mixed in well, add mozzarella cheese, 1 cup cheddar cheese, pepper and green onion. Pour mixture into a casserole dish and bake at 350 degrees for 30 minutes or until bubbly. Remove from oven and place ½ cup of grits into each bacon cup. Top with remaining cheddar cheese and serve.

Bloody Mary Pie

5-6 Roma tomatoes, sliced or 12-14 ripe cherry tomatoes

1 teaspoon salt

1 deep dish pie crust

1 cup shredded sharp cheddar cheese

½ cup shredded mozzarella cheese

½ cup grated Parmesan

¾ cup mayonnaise

¼ cup fresh basil, chopped

¼ cup green onion, chopped

1 teaspoon minced garlic

½ teaspoon pepper

Preheat oven to 375 degrees. Line a baking sheet with paper towels and place tomatoes in a single layer. Sprinkle with salt to remove excess juice. Bake pie crust for 10 minutes. In a medium bowl, mix together the sharp cheddar cheese, mozzarella cheese, grated Parmesan and mayonnaise. Firmly press the tomatoes with paper towels to soak up juice then place them in the bottom of the pie crust and top with basil, green onion, minced garlic and pepper. Then spread the cheese mixture evenly across the tomato filling. Reduce heat to 350 degrees and bake for 30 minutes. Remove from oven and allow to rest for 10 minutes before slicing.

Larissa's Sinful Twist

5-6 Roma tomatoes, sliced

1 teaspoon celery salt, divided

1 deep dish pie crust

1 cup shredded sharp cheddar cheese

1 cup shredded mozzarella cheese

½ cup grated Parmesan

¾ cup mayonnaise

1 teaspoon minced garlic

3 teaspoons Frank's Red Hot Sauce or tabasco

1 ¼ teaspoon Worcestershire sauce

¼ teaspoon red pepper flakes (or to taste)

¼ cup fresh basil, chopped

¼ cup green onion, chopped

½ teaspoon black pepper

Green Olive Tapenade

Preheat oven to 375 degrees. Line a baking sheet with paper towels and place tomatoes in a single layer. Sprinkle with ¾ teaspoon celery salt to remove excess juice. Bake pie crust for 10 minutes. In a medium bowl, mix together the 3 cheeses, mayonnaise, garlic, hot sauce, Worcestershire, and red pepper flakes. Firmly press the tomatoes with paper towels to soak up juice then place them in the bottom of the pie crust and top with basil, green onion, ¼ teaspoon celery salt, and black pepper. Then spread the cheese mixture evenly across the tomato filling. Reduce heat to 350 degrees and bake for 30 minutes. Top with Green Olive Tapenade.

Green Olive Tapenade

¼ cup olive oil

1 clove garlic

1 teaspoon fresh lemon juice

1 tablespoon capers, drained

1 cup green olives

½ cup green olives stuffed with pimentos

Place all ingredients in a food processor and pulse until coarsely chopped. If you don't have a food processor, mince garlic and olives, and then stir all ingredients together.

Pumpkin Spice Loaf with Spiced Icing

1 cup sugar

1 tablespoon pumpkin pie spice

8 tablespoons (1 stick) butter, melted

1 (8 count) can flaky layer biscuits

1 can pumpkin filling

Preheat oven to 350 degrees. Spray 9 x 5-inch loaf pan with cooking spray. On a large plate, mix together sugar and pumpkin pie spice. In a separate bowl add the butter. Separate dough into 8 biscuits. Separate each biscuit into 2 layers, making a total of 16 biscuit rounds. Dredge each biscuit in the melted butter, then dip each side into the sugar mixture. On a second large plate, place 4 biscuit rounds a time. Top with 1-2 tablespoons of pie filling. Stack biscuits in 4 piles of 4 biscuits each. Place stacks on their sides in a row in loaf pan, making sure sides without filling are on both ends touching pan. Bake 50 minutes or until loaf is deep golden brown and center is baked through. Cool 10 minutes. Top with Spiced Icing to serve.

Spiced Icing

8 tablespoons (1 stick) butter, softened

1 (8 ounce) package cream cheese, softened

1 teaspoon vanilla extract

1 teaspoon pumpkin pie spice

3 cups powdered sugar

In a large bowl, using a hand mixer, combine butter, cream cheese, vanilla and pumpkin pie spice until blended. Add powdered sugar one cup at a time until all 3 cups are blended.

Egg in a HellHole Avocado Toast

1 medium ripe avocado, peeled and seeded

2 tablespoons lime juice

2 tablespoons green onion, chopped

¼ teaspoon salt

¼ teaspoon pepper

2 slices Texas toast

2 tablespoons butter

2 large eggs

In a medium bowl, add the avocado, lime juice, green onion, salt, and pepper. Coarsely mash the avocado with a fork and stir to combine, then cover with plastic wrap and set aside. Cut a 3-inch circle from the center of each bread slice with a cookie cutter or glass. In a large non-stick skillet, heat the butter over medium-low heat to melt. Add the bread and bread rounds, and cook until golden brown on the first side, about 1 to 2 minutes. Flip everything over, crack one egg into the hole of each piece of bread, and season eggs with salt and pepper. Cook until eggs are as set as desired, about 3 to 6 minutes. The bread rounds need to be removed after 2 minutes. Remove the egg in a hole from the skillet as soon as the egg is cooked to desired doneness. Evenly spread the avocado mixture over the bread and bread rounds and serve immediately.

Maple Sausage and Waffle Casserole

8 frozen waffles

1 pound maple sausage, cooked and crumbled

1 cup cheddar cheese

6 eggs

1 cup milk

¼ cup maple syrup

Pinch of cinnamon

Maple syrup (for topping)

Tear waffles into bite size pieces and place half on the bottom of an 8 x 8-inch cake pan. Top with half of the sausage and half of the cheese. Repeat this process to finish building casserole. In a large bowl, mix together the eggs, milk, syrup and cinnamon. Pour over casserole and cover. Refrigerate for at least an hour to overnight. Bake at 325 degrees for 45 minutes. Serve with maple syrup, if desired.

Breakfast Burrito

1 batch Fried Chicken Nuggets

1 batch Thin Pancakes

2 cups sharp cheddar cheese

1 batch Honey Sriracha Sauce

Place 3-4 chicken nuggets in the center of a thin pancake. Top with ¼ cup cheddar cheese and Honey Sriracha Sauce. Fold into a burrito and enjoy.

Fried Chicken Nuggets

Oil for frying

6-8 boneless, skinless chicken breast tenders

3 cups flour

1 tablespoon seasoning salt

3 eggs

½ cup milk

Heat oil in a deep fryer or Dutch oven to 350 degrees. Cut the chicken tenders into 1-inch chunks. Mix together the flour and seasoning salt. Then whisk together the eggs and milk. Place the chicken in the egg mixture. Dredge 6 chicken pieces at a time in flour, shaking off excess. Fry the chicken pieces in the oil until golden brown, about 4-6 minutes. Remove from oil and drain on a paper bag. Continue with remaining chicken.

Thin Pancakes (burrito)

2 eggs

½ tablespoon sugar

2 cups milk

¼ teaspoon salt

1 ¼ cups flour

3-4 tablespoons butter

In a large bowl, beat together eggs and sugar. Add the milk, salt and flour and mix until smooth. Allow batter to rest for 10 minutes. In a large non-stick skillet, melt ½ tablespoon butter over medium heat. Pour 2-3 tablespoons of batter into the skillet and tilt skillet around so the batter spreads out to make a 6-7 inch pancake. Cook for 1 minute on each side or until golden brown. Remove from skillet and repeat with remaining batter. Makes 8-10 thin pancakes.

Honey Sriracha Sauce

1 cup honey
¼ cup mayonnaise
3 tablespoons sriracha

Add all ingredients to a small blender and mix on low for about 1 minute.

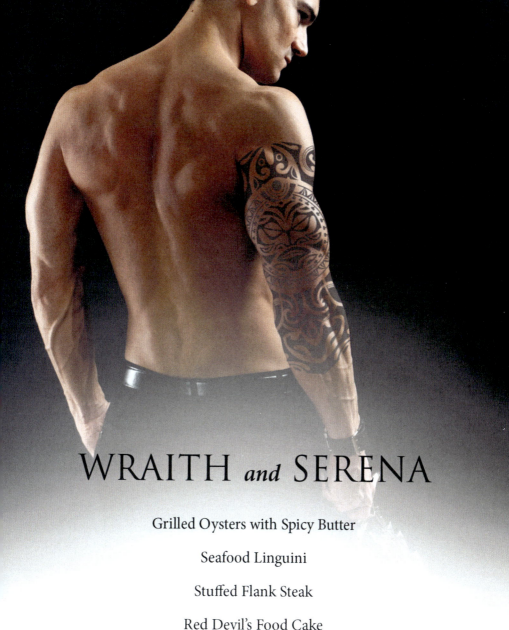

WRAITH and SERENA

Grilled Oysters with Spicy Butter

Seafood Linguini

Stuffed Flank Steak

Red Devil's Food Cake

Steak Bruschetta with Onion Jam

Bananas Foster Crème Brulee

Caprese Chicken with Balsamic Glaze

Sex is good, but not as good as fresh, sweet corn. ~ Garrison Keillor
Just what the floof is he doing with that corn? ~ Wraith

WRAITH AND SERENA

When Serena thought back on the highlights of her life, she always found that there were too many to list. Sure, there had been a lot of tragedy, but the good things far outnumbered the bad.

The day she'd become a vampire was one of the best. So was the day she bonded with her mate, Wraith, an incubus who also happened to be a vampire. And the day Wraith's brother Shade brought them Wraith's infant son, born in the hospital run by Wraith and his brothers. It didn't matter that Serena hadn't given birth to Talon, who they affectionately called Stewie. He was her son, and she'd loved every minute of her seven years of motherhood.

She and Wraith hadn't explained the circumstances of Stewie's birth to him yet, but they needed to do it soon, before he figured it out on his own. His world — and his knowledge base — was expanding thanks to the friends he'd made at the special academy for underworlder children in Switzerland. The academy, hidden in plain sight in a Bern neighborhood, was easily accessible via Harrowgates, making it just a ten minute walk from their house in New York.

Humans — and more importantly, The Aegis, a demon-slaying organization that made no distinction between good underworld beings and evil ones — believed the academy was an elite boarding school for rich kids, and so far, it had been a good fit for Stewie. Shade and Runa's triplets and Eidolon and Tayla's son went there as well, and Lore and Idess's son would start next year.

Right now, though, Idess was on her way over to drop off little Mace for Serena to watch while Idess and Lore enjoyed a night out.

In fact, when Serena heard the front door open, she thought it might be Idess, but a moment later Wraith's booming voice echoed through the house.

"Hey, sexy vampiress, I'm home!" He swept into the kitchen where she was making Stewie a snack, looking like sin and sex in a tall, blond package. In three strides he crossed the room and swept her into his arms. "Hello, mate."

She laughed and gave him a kiss. "You're in a good mood."

He grinned, flashing fangs, his blue eyes twinkling. "That's because I cured cancer today."

"You." She raised a skeptical eyebrow. Wraith liked *causing* medical maladies. Fixing them wasn't his thing. "*You* cured cancer."

"Hell, yeah. It's a rare form of lunecarcinoma that affects werebears." He released her and propped his hip against the counter, his stance relaxed, but inside he was always coiled tight with deadly energy, ready to leap into danger at a moment's notice. "I mean, I found a clove in Sheoul last year that Eidolon turned into a treatment. But I did the important part." He shot her his patented roguish wink and smirk that had drawn her in from the moment she met him all those years ago in Egypt.

"Daddy?" Stewie's dark head popped up from the table, where he'd had his face buried in twelfth-grade science books. At seven, he had the reading comprehension of a high school senior and the career focus of a thirty-year-old.

Wraith pushed off the counter toward his son. "Hey, little dude. I didn't even see you there. You doing homework?"

Stewie ignored the question and blurted out one of his own. "You cured cancer? For real?"

"Yes, he did," Serena said as she turned back to the Mini Chicken Gyros she was going to taste test on Stewie before she made a few dozen of them for Cara's upcoming baby shower. "Aren't you proud of him?"

Stewie's head bobbed excitedly. "You gonna be a doctor now? Uncle Eidolon would let you, I bet. He says they always need help at the hospital."

"No way, kiddo." Wraith ruffled Stew's hair playfully. "Someone's gotta find all the rare stuff your uncle needs to heal patients."

Disappointment practically leaked out of Stew's pores as he slumped back in his seat. "I guess."

Stewie had worshipped Eidolon practically from the moment he was born, and he wanted to follow in his uncle's footsteps. Nothing would make him happier than seeing his father do the same.

Wraith didn't seem to notice Stew's change of mood as he reached into the pocket of his favorite worn leather jacket. "Hey, I got something cool. Tickets to *Monster Mash & Demon Trash* this weekend. All species of underworlders battling it out in over a dozen themed arenas. Awesome, huh?"

Serena huffed, hands on her hips. "I thought we were going to talk about this first. You know I don't like the violence."

"Most of the time no one dies," Wraith protested. "And it's perfectly safe for spectators."

"No thanks." Stewie hunkered down with his books again. "Mom and Uncle Eidolon said I could watch a surgery this weekend."

"Seriously?" Wraith shot her an accusatory look. "You think watching a bloody surgery is okay, but lion shifters versus Ragenor demons on an obstacle course is bad?"

Um...yes.

"The obstacle courses have moving, razor sharp blades, pools of lava, and bear traps." She plated two gyros for Stewie and set aside the rest for Wraith and Mace. "The surgery Eidolon invited him to see is a minor outpatient procedure on a child, and E thought Stewie could comfort the boy."

She felt Wraith's heat on her back as he reached around her to snag a gyro. "Why would E do that?"

"To encourage Stewie's interest in medicine." She turned her head to give him a peck on the cheek. "Eidolon's a doctor. It's not like he's teaching him how to be an assassin or something."

Even the assassins in the family wouldn't do that.

"Eidolon has his own kid to screw up," Wraith muttered as he dipped his gyro into the bowl of tzatziki sauce she'd made earlier. "He needs to keep his surgical gloves off mine. Besides, Stewie is only seven. He'll change his mind."

"No I won't," Stew called out.

Wraith waggled his eyebrows at his son. "Just wait until your mom decides you're old enough to go one on of our artifact hunts. It's exciting. It'll awaken your Indiana Jones spirit. You'll see."

Stewie rolled his eyes and looked back down at his books.

"Hey." Serena held out the plate of gyros to Stewie. "Why don't you take your snack to your room and clean it up before Mace gets here? I'll bring you something to drink in a minute."

Scowling, Stewie took the plate. "Why is he coming over? I don't want to play with him. He's a baby."

"Listen to your mother." Wraith palmed another gyro. "And your cousin is four. He's not a baby."

"He's not my cousin." Stewie slammed his book shut and shoved to his feet. "He's my *brother*, and I hate him."

"Stew!" Serena spun around from the cabinet she'd opened to get a cup. "That's not nice. You don't mean that."

"Whatever," Stewie muttered as he gathered his books and stormed out of the kitchen.

Wraith started after him, but Serena stopped him with a gentle grip on his forearm. "Let him go. I think he just needs time to process."

"He's known that Mace is his biological brother for a month." Wraith frowned as he stared down the hall where Stew had gone. "He should have processed by now."

She cringed as Stewie's door slammed. He'd always had his father's temper, but he'd never mistreated a door.

"He's only seven," she reminded Wraith. "I know he acts older in a lot of ways, but he *is* a child, and he figured out on his own that Mace is more than his cousin."

Wraith sank heavily onto a barstool. "We explained how it happened when he asked us about it, though. He knows the whole thing about Lore being sterile. He said he understood."

And what a fun conversation *that* had been. As a human, Serena had different ideas about parenting than Wraith, a sex demon did. She hadn't been prepared for the rather frank way Wraith had explained how he, Shade, and Eidolon had, with their mates' help, "hand-mixed some baby batter" so Idess could conceive.

"But it's like he blames me for something." Wraith looked down at the *dermoire* on his arm, a series of glyphs every Seminus demon was born with, Stewie included. "He acts like he hates me lately."

Serena wanted to tell Wraith he was wrong, but Stewie had been acting out a lot since he'd found out that Mace was his brother. Everyone had assured her it was just a phase, and she had to believe that, because she hated seeing Wraith and Stewie in pain.

"He just needs time." She tenderly pushed a lock of his shoulder-length hair back from his handsome face, loving how he leaned into her touch. "He feels like we betrayed him by not telling him. He'll come around."

Wraith again looked down the hall after Stew. "I hope you're right," he said, but the troubled expression on his face said he didn't think she was.

Wraith spent the next two days trying to convince Stewie to go to *Monster Mash & Demon Trash* with him, but his son was dead set on spending the day at the hospital with Eidolon.

What the hell? How had Stew not inherited Wraith's adventurous gene? Instead he'd gotten Eidolon's starched sense of duty, and the more Wraith tried to bond with him, the more he pulled away. Serena kept insisting that Wraith needed to back off and let Stew come around on his own, but Wraith wasn't exactly known for his patience.

Maybe he needed a distraction.

He eyed Serena as she bent over to make the bed, and yep, there was the distraction he needed. Gaze locked on the way her faded jeans hugged her softly rounded backside and slender thighs, he moved toward her, his body hardening with every step.

Yes, he was a Seminus demon, a rare breed of incubus that required sex to survive like humans required oxygen. But with Serena, it wasn't *just* sex he needed. He needed *her*. She'd saved his life in a million different ways. Hell, she saved his life every time she had sex with him.

Serena fluffed his pillow…the pillow he was going to use to brace her hips when he…*oh, yeah*, he could practically feel his fangs scraping over skin still sensitive from this morning.

They'd spent a lot of time in bed lately. Well, not any more than usual, but for some reason it felt like that was all they did when they were together.

He slowed, suddenly disturbed by that thought.

They used to hunt for artifacts together, but lately Serena had been spending time with Cara to help with the pending arrival of the baby.

She'd spent a *lot* of time helping to prepare for the baby.

He froze in his tracks, his objective forgotten. As a vampire, Serena couldn't give birth. Did that bother her? Was that why she was with Cara so much when Stewie was at school?

Serena straightened and turned to him. "Wraith? Is everything okay?"

He blinked. "Yeah. Why?"

"Because I thought you were going to throw me down on the bed and ravage me." She smiled, showing a pearly hint of her sexy fangs. She'd been a pretty badass human when he'd first set out to seduce her, but with vampire strength and speed, now she was like a superhero badass. So floofing hot. "But instead you're standing there like a zombie. What's going on?"

Oh, I was just wondering if maybe you resented the fact that you can't have a baby.

Probably best not to just blurt that out. They definitely needed to talk, but maybe after they got out and did something. Something besides sex.

He'd probably just become the only Seminus demon in the history of incubi to have that thought.

"Wraith?" Serena prompted.

Think quick. "I changed my mind about meeting Thanatos and Regan for cocktails tonight."

She blinked in surprise. "I thought you said Eidolon needed you to hunt down some sort of Oni relic."

Screw Eidolon. He was trying to drag Stewie to the Dark Side. Okay, yeah, there were worse things his brother could do than foster Stewie's interest in the medical profession, but Wraith felt like being petty. At least he admitted it. That had to count toward something, right? Like, maturity points.

He was totally next-level mature.

"E can wait until tomorrow," he said. "We need to hang out with friends and be social."

And how crazy was it that he considered Thanatos, the Horseman known as Death, to be a friend? His best friend, in fact. They'd hit it off from the beginning, and Regan and Serena had developed a close relationship, as well.

"Really?" Grinning, she checked her watch. "I'll get Runa to watch Stewie."

It only took them forty-five minutes to get in a playful quickie in the shower and drop Stew off with Shade and Runa. A few minutes after that, they took a Harrowgate that delivered them within two blocks of one of their favorite watering holes, a hard-to-find underground bar in Bruges. The place was dark, moody, and had the atmosphere of a Gothic tomb. Best of all, it was rarely packed with tourists.

Regan and Thanatos were already seated at a table near the back with a cheese and meat platter, and Thanatos, bless his apocalyptic heart, had a beer waiting for him. Regan had ordered a hard cider for Serena, earning a hug before they all sat down.

"It's good to see you, man." Thanatos, wearing a sweater the color of the Guinness in his hand, lifted his glass in salute. "Been awhile."

"Wraith has been busy with work." Serena palmed Wraith's thigh under the table and gave him an affectionate squeeze. Her excitement at getting a night out told Wraith they needed to do this more often.

"Uh-huh." Thanatos scoffed. "Wraith doesn't work. He hunts treasure."

Wraith knocked back half his beer. "No, it's true. I cured cancer, in fact." He smirked at Thanatos. "What have you done lately? Haunted cemeteries?"

The Horseman snorted. "Now I remember why it's been awhile."

Laughing, Regan took Thanatos's hand. "He's been teaching Logan how to ice fish."

"I can't wait until Amber is old enough," Thanatos said. "Then we can all go fishing."

"All?" Regan gave her mate a *you're delusional* look. "I think ice fishing sounds like it would make for a wonderful father-offspring weekend."

"While Mom spends quiet time binge-watching shows she's missed," Serena added.

Regan clinked glasses with Serena. "You said it, sister."

"I think ice fishing sounds great." Wraith wrapped his arm around Serena. "I mean, screw the fishing part. But warming up in a cold shanty with your mate? I can deal with that."

"I'm with you," Serena said, snuggling against him. "Fishing isn't my thing, but I'd let you keep me warm." She dragged a playful finger down the center of the Four Ponies of the Apocalypse T-shirt he liked to wear to taunt Thanatos. "I love it when you get all romantic."

"Wraith?" Regan plucked a cube of cheese off the plate. "Romantic? Bullshit."

"No, really, I am," Wraith insisted. "Just last week I brought Serena a corrupt politician to eat."

Serena nodded. "It was so sweet. When I was done, he told the loser to confess his sins to the public or Wraith would find him again."

"Dude." Than nodded approvingly. "That's awesome."

Regan just shook her head and signaled the bartender for another cider. "Romance is in the eye of the beholder, I guess."

Serena took a sip of her drink. "What do you consider romantic?"

Regan appeared to think on that. Finally she said, "Sometimes Than puts the kids to bed, runs a bubble bath for me, and while I'm soaking he reads to me."

That sounded super lame to Wraith, but Serena perked up.

"Reads? Like what?"

"Depends," Regan said with a shrug. "Sometimes it's something light and funny. Sometimes it's one of the thousand accounts of the exploits of the Four Horsemen."

Thanatos's weird yellow eyes went heavy-lidded as he leaned back in his chair and eyed his mate like he was hungry and she was a steak. "Tell them your favorite reading material."

Even in the shadowy darkness in the crypt-like atmosphere of the bar, Regan's blush bloomed bright. "I like it when he gives me a glass of wine and reads a steamy romance." She shot him a seductive smile. "I always know it's romance novel night when he gives me red wine."

"I like the way red wine turns your cheeks pink and makes you adventurous," he purred.

"You think I'm not adventurous?"

"Oh, you're game for anything." Thanatos fed her a piece of cheese, placing it gently on her tongue. "But my bold warrior isn't so bold with the dirty talk."

Regan's eyes sparked with the light of battle. "You're asking for it now. I'll take that as a challenge."

"Good. Wanna go home and challenge me?"

That was a total eye-roller right there. "Are you two done?" Wraith asked.

Thanatos hid his smile in his glass. "Sorry. With two little ones we don't get a lot of alone time."

"Who's watching the ponies while you're here?" Serena asked, using the term Regan often used to refer to their kids.

"Cujo and the vampires," Regan replied.

Between Thanatos's vampire servants and Cujo, a hellhound given to their son Logan as a puppy, nothing was going to get near those kids.

"Cujo and the vampires, huh?" Wraith mused. "Sounds like a rock band."

"You're not wrong," Thanatos muttered. "Thanks to Limos and her brilliant idea to give Logan a drums set for his birthday."

"I can't wait to pay her back," Regan said. "As soon as Keilani is old enough, I'm getting her a tuba and a hellhound puppy that'll howl when she plays it."

Wraith had heard Cujo howl, and the sound was definitely an ear-splitter. Stewie had asked for a hellhound puppy for his birthday a couple of years ago, but even if Serena hadn't put her foot down on that one, Cujo's vocalizations -- and his potential for eating people -- had given Wraith second thoughts.

He ordered another beer, and they all sat around the table for the next couple of hours catching up and talking about Ares and Cara's upcoming baby shower. Finally, when the bartender announced he'd be closing the joint, they drained their glasses and headed for a dark alley where Thanatos could gate them all home.

Wraith didn't envy the Horsemen – their lives had been even more floofed up than Wraith's, and they still had centuries of prophecy to deal with. But damn, their ability to open gates to anywhere was one Wraith would kill to have.

As they rounded the corner on their way to their usual spot, a group of people started toward them. To the casual observer, they appeared to be human.

But as the hair on Wraith's neck stood up, he slowed, pulling Serena to a stop at the same time Than and Regan came to a halt.

The group of eleven underworlders, a mix of demons and shifters, if Wraith's senses were working right, stopped a few yards away.

"Looks like we eat well tonight, friends," the one in front said, and Regan barked out a laugh.

"You idiots chose the wrong people to floof with," she said.

The lead idiot hissed, his mouth filling with sharp teeth. "You're outnumbered, *idiot*."

Wraith snorted. "That's like telling the Avengers that they're outnumbered."

One of the creeps in the back of the pack snickered. "Yeah? And what Avenger are you?"

"Me? Not to brag, but I'm kind of invincible. You know, like Thor." He looked over at Serena. "Right, babe?"

She gave him a thumbs' up, and a "Sure, hon. Thor."

He loved how she humored him.

Wraith gestured to Thanatos. "He's Iron Man."

Thanatos played along and skimmed his fingers across the crescent scar on his throat. Instantly a suit of armor clacked into place, covering him from head to toe. Wraith smirked at the uneasiness that filtered through the group of scumbags. An uneasiness that grew when the souls kept prisoner inside Thanatos's armor began to writhe around his feet, shadowy wraiths that wanted out. That wanted to kill.

It was creepy as floof.

Casually, while the pack of idiots were focused on his inane Avengers talk, he palmed one of the blades at his hip with one hand and gestured to Serena with the other.

"She can shoot a bow like Hawkeye and move like Wasp." He jerked his chin toward Regan. "She's a professional demon slayer. The Black Widow of our group. And Iron Man, here? His name is Death. He's literally Death. And I almost singlehandedly closed the gates of hell and saved the world. There might be fewer of us, but I promise, you are the ones who are outnumbered."

Regan heaved a long-suffering sigh. "Do you realize that every time you meet someone new, you find a way to bring up the fact that you saved the world?"

"It's true," Than said, and Serena gave him an apologetic nod of agreement.

"What can I say?" Wraith asked with a shrug. "I need the adulation. My ego is fragile."

"Shut up," one of the newcomers growled, his voice becoming slurred as he and his toadies began to morph into their true, ugly-ass forms. "We don't like our dinner to talk back to us."

Oh, yeah, Wraith thought as he settled into a fighting stance.

This was gonna be fun.

It had been a long time since Serena and Wraith had fought side-by-side against an enemy. Family life had kind of put a damper on some of their more intense adventures, so this...this was a throwback to their roots, a reminder of how they'd met, and how they'd fallen in love.

And as she crunched a flying roundhouse kick into the throat of one of their attackers, she wasn't surprised to see Wraith peel away from the black-horned demon he'd just decked to back her up. In tandem, the way they practiced at the UGH gym, they took the bastard down. Wraith devastated the fang-toothed monster with a series of blows to the upper body as she spun, delivering sweeping kicks to soft spots and vulnerable joints in the demon's legs.

Regan and Thanatos were working together as well, mowing through the group of scumbags with the ease of a freshly sharpened blade through grass. In less than three minutes, the four of them were standing in a circle, back to back, the enemies lying around them like broken sacks of grain.

"Well, that was fun. A little too easy, but fun," Thanatos said, but his lips were turned down in a troubled frown that drew a scowl from Regan.

"What is it?" she asked.

The scorpion tattoo on Thanatos's neck had come to life, its tail whipping around as if stinging him. "Something's...wrong. The souls I released aren't being gathered by *griminions* after their kills."

Serena tried not to shiver, but the creepiness of Thanatos's soul-killer gift weirded her out. Regan had told her that the shadowy souls would fly around until the Grim Reaper's *griminions* came to collect them, which usually didn't take more than a few seconds.

"Wait," she said. "Didn't you say earlier that the gates to Sheoul-gra are closed? Isn't that where the souls are taken?"

Thanatos turned his intense yellow eyes on her, and if she wasn't a friend, she would have shrunk back. "Yes," his deep voice rumbled. "I'd forgotten about that. Dammit, Azagoth had better get his shit together."

He turned back to the alleyway where the bodies of the dead demons were caving in on themselves, disintegrating into bubbling puddles before poofing into fine ash flakes. Within seconds, there would be no trace of them left at all.

Thanatos cursed as even the ash flakes fizzled out of existence. "Can we not go even a decade without a crisis? Floof it, I'd take even a couple of *years*."

"What's been going on?" Serena asked. She'd been *so* out of the loop lately.

Regan finished searching the alley for her throwing knives and tucked them into her purse. "There have been rumblings of a new coup planned against Revenant."

"And there's been a spate of angel assassinations, most of them Memitim," Thanatos said. "Before the near-apocalypse a few years ago, we used to be able to go centuries at a time without large-scale incidents of demonic turmoil."

"What's different now?" Serena asked, turning to give a couple of drunk humans at the end of the alley a look that said they'd be smart to take another route. Wisely, they took her wordless advice.

Thanatos waited until the humans were gone and then turned his attention back to Serena, although, like Wraith, he never stopped watching for trouble. "My theory is that in the past, organized demonic activity didn't have much of a point. Yes, Satan always had his minions out looking for ways to corrupt humans and recruit disenfranchised angels and commit general mayhem, but most high-level activity was ultimately done with the goal of starting the End of Days."

"But we won," Wraith said. "We floofing beat the Apocalypse. Satan is imprisoned."

"Only for a thousand years," Thanatos reminded him. "When he is loosed, the real End of Days will be upon us."

An ominous silence settled over them like a shroud.

Then Regan laughed.

Thanatos leveled a flat look at his mate. "Armageddon amuses you?"

"No, I just think it's funny how you go all medieval-sounding when you get angry or serious. All you're missing is some thees and thous."

"*Thee* end of the world is pretty serious," Than muttered a little defensively.

Which Serena thought was funny. The guy was a seven-foot-tall warrior decked out in massive bone-plate armor and covered in 3-D tattoos depicting scenes of death, and he got as pouty as Stewie sometimes.

"Oh, come on," Regan said. "We have plenty of time to prepare. Not to mention the fact that since we beat the prophesied demonic apocalypse, we only have to worry about the Biblical one. And the Horsemen fight for good in that one."

"We might be on the side of good, but that doesn't mean we'll *be* good. Psychopaths make the best assassins, after all. When our Seals break, we may still become monsters."

"Whoa, there, Debbie Downer," Wraith drawled. "Nothing like doomsday talk to end a night, huh?"

"Oh, give me a break," Serena teased. "You love this kind of thing."

Wraith grinned. "Yeah."

Thanatos cursed again, his eyes glowing eerily until Regan took his gauntleted hand. "I'm sure Azagoth will open Sheoul-gra to souls again soon. Try not to worry about it. Whatever the souls you released do now will not be your fault."

Thanatos didn't look mollified in the least.

"Hey," Wraith said in a cheery voice Serena knew was meant to distract. "Why don't we find a good breakfast joint? I know this restaurant in Hawaii that whips up some crazy good Spam omelets."

"Another time, demon," Thanatos said as he opened a gate to Wraith and Serena's backyard in New York. "We'll see you on Ares's island on for the baby shower?"

"Of course," Serena said. "We wouldn't miss it."

They said their goodbyes, and then Serena and Wraith stepped through the gate, which closed behind them.

"Well, that was an interesting evening," she said as they mounted the steps to the back deck.

"Yeah. It was one of the more normal ones we've had with them."

She laughed at the truth in that. Weirdness followed the Horsemen everywhere they went. "It's still pretty early...want to hunt?"

"Don't we have to pick up Stewie?" He held open the back door for her, and as she entered, she palmed his muscular chest and playfully dragged her hand down to the waistband of his jeans.

"Runa said she'd bring him home tomorrow. We have all night."

"That's what I love to hear."

He scooped her up as if she weighed no more than a pint of cider and carried her through the house. He nuzzled her neck as he strode toward the bedroom, his fangs scraping her jugular possessively. Oh, she couldn't wait to feel them sink deep.

"Thank you," she whispered as he set her down next to the bed.

"For what?"

"For giving me a distraction."

He pulled back and looked down her, puzzled. "A distraction?"

"From worrying about Stewie." She kicked off her shoes. "I've been really freaked out about telling him the truth about his birth."

"You worry too much. And it should be *me* thanking *you*." His warm hands slid beneath her top and began a slow, torturous slide upward. His touch, gentle but commanding, was a sensual weapon that he wielded like a master. He could get her to do anything, and she would never complain about that.

She sighed as his fingers breached the fabric of her bra. "Mmm...for what?"

Dipping his head, he brushed his lips along the curve of her ear, his hot breath fanning her skin and making her shiver. "For being such a great mother to my son."

She froze, unsure how to take that. Maybe she was being too sensitive, but something about the way he'd said that struck a nerve, and she jerked out of his grip.

"Excuse me? Stewie is my son too."

"I know," Wraith said, reaching for her again. "Now, if we can just get horizontal..."

For some reason, that just pissed her off. No, not for "some reason." She knew exactly what had done it. He was dismissing her concerns, prioritizing sex over them. Sure, he was a sex demon, and he'd die without it, but she also knew when he was in desperate need and when he wasn't.

Right now...he wasn't.

"Wait." She backed up, not ready to give in yet. This was too important and she was way too stressed about it. "Why did you say I'm a great mother to your son?"

He frowned. "You just said you were worried about how he'd react to the fact that you didn't give birth to him."

"But is that what you really think? That I'm just taking care of him because he's yours and I'm mated to you?"

Outside the house, a truck rumbled by, filling the awkward silence until finally Wraith said, "It's not that. It's just that I noticed how much time you've spent with Cara. I thought maybe it's because you can't have a baby of your own."

"Floofing excuse me?" she repeated, her temper hitting the flashpoint. "I'm spending time with Cara because she's my friend. I don't need to hang out with a pregnant lady because I have feelings of inadequacy or some shit." She jammed her feet into her shoes. "I need to take a walk."

"Where are you going?"

"I'll be at Cara's. You know, wishing I could be pregnant."

"I didn't mean it, Serena."

She paused and blew out a long, calming breath. "I know." She did. And she knew she was being irrational. And maybe, just maybe, he was on to something and she didn't want to admit it. She wasn't sure, but what she was sure of was that she needed a little time to think, and she couldn't do it around him. "I just need some time alone. I'll be fine. See you later."

Before she could reconsider, she snagged her purse and got the hell out of there.

Serena hadn't come home last night.

Wraith had been forced to dose himself with the sexual suppressant drug that Eidolon had developed a while back, and then he'd prowled around the house for hours. Just as he was about to head to Ares's island to bring her back, she'd texted.

I know you're probably pacing around the house like a caged tiger, but I promise I'm fine. I'm not mad at you. I just needed to step back and think about things a little. Cara helped me get my head on straight. I'm going to return the favor and help her out today, but I'll be home this evening. I can bring something home for dinner.

Tonight? Floof that. He wasn't waiting until tonight to see her. He'd spent the early morning thinking about why she'd been so angry, and only when he put himself in her shoes — personal growth, floof, yeah — had he realized why she might be so touchy about Wraith's shit-poor choice of words. She was already worried about how Stewie would react to the truth of his birth, but then to have her fears of rejection reinforced by Wraith's idiotic phrasing...yeah, he could see why she'd been hurt.

Usually when he floofed up, he made it better with charm and sex. But when he thought back to the bedroom and how it all started, it seemed like he might need to pull a new trick out of his bag of *forgive me* tactics.

Weird. He'd always thought sex could fix *everything*.

Son of a bitch, he was growing as a person, wasn't he? And Shade said it would never happen. Asshole.

Shoving his personal revelations aside to revisit...*never*, he checked with Runa to make sure she could keep Stewie for a couple more hours, and then he headed to the neighborhood Harrowgate. Few knew about Ares and Cara's Greek island, and even fewer could access it, but the Horseman had given his most trusted friends and allies the key to the island's lone Harrowgate.

Wraith stepped out into the mid-afternoon sunshine, but before he even got to the main cobblestoned path leading to the mansion, Ares intercepted him, decked out in cargo shorts and a cheery green shirt that didn't fool anyone into thinking he was an easygoing dude.

The guy's Horseman name was War, and fittingly, he was built like a tank. His face was as hard as one as well, and Wraith knew that from experience.

"I wouldn't." Ares's voice rumbled like the waves in the distance.

"Wouldn't what?"

"Bother Serena."

"*Bother* her?"

"You know what I mean, demon." The sea breeze stirred Ares's short, reddish-brown hair as he stopped in front of Wraith. "Our females are strong and independent. They come home when they want to."

"Big words, man. But you know if the situation were reversed, you'd throw Cara over your shoulder and haul her back home."

One massive shoulder rolled in a shrug. "I'd think about it," he admitted. "And then I'd remember that every hellhound in existence would bite me if she told them to." He sighed. "Look, I don't know what's going on, but I'm guessing you floofed up big time. Right?"

"Maybe."

"What did you do?"

"I said something that implied Serena was basically nothing but a babysitter for my kid."

Ares winced. "Dude."

Wraith swore he could actually *feel* Ares's pity. The old Wraith would have gotten defensive and sarcastic and called him a horse's ass. Personal Growth Wraith was going to listen to the ancient warrior and merely keep the sarcasm on deck in case of emergencies.

For a long moment, Ares stood there, his gaze turned inward. "I said something similar to my first wife, except she *did* give birth to our children. But I was an arrogant hardass and it was a different time, when a mother's influence on boys was considered to contribute to softness." He shook his head. "I was such a fool."

Ares's entire family had been killed by demons, and his sorrow radiated off him in waves, even though it had happened thousands of years ago. Wraith hadn't believed pain could last that long, but now that he had a mate and son of his own, he no longer doubted.

"What did you do to make it up to her?"

Shame cast shadows in Ares's eyes. "Nothing. So here's what you do. Learn from my stupidity. Plan something nice for Serena. Something she won't expect, that's outside your comfort zone. Show her that without her, you wouldn't have a family." Wraith must have had a skeptical look on his face, because the Horseman snorted. "You kidding me, demon? I know you. She'd be fine without you, but without her? You'd be dead. I'm willing to bet that she's the glue that holds all of you together, right?"

Wraith had never really thought about it like that before, but the horse's ass had a point. Without her he wouldn't be who he was...assuming he would even be alive. Either way, Shade and Runa would be raising his son. Serena was absolutely the reason Stewie was a stable, happy kid and the reason Wraith had a family at all.

"You're right," Wraith admitted with a shrug. "Had to happen sooner or later."

Ares snorted again. "I'm always right."

"I have a feeling Cara would disagree."

"No," Ares said, "she wouldn't. Because we're not going to tell her I said that."

Wraith laughed. He'd known the Horsemen for years now, and it cracked him up that these warriors of legend and prophecy could take down entire armies...but they could be felled by a solitary female. No mystical armor was a defense against the love of a mate and the draw of family life.

The reminder was a welcome one for Personal Growth Wraith, and Ares's advice was even more welcome.

Now it was time to turn that advice into action. Action Serena would never see coming, because while very little existed outside Wraith's comfort zone, there was one thing he didn't do. Ever.

He was going to cook.

Butterflies stirred in Serena's belly as she opened the front door.

But the moment she stepped into the house, the nervous butterflies turned ravenous as she was overcome by the incredible mingled aromas of chocolate and buttery seafood.

"Whatever you're doing in the kitchen," she called out, "it smells amazing. You must have picked up dinner at the Bits & Bites down the street."

"Nope," Wraith said, poking his head around the kitchen corner. "I cooked. No shit."

Whoa. He never cooked. He could barely make a bowl of Top Ramen. "You...cooked." She spoke as she walked down the hall. "All by yourself? No way."

She rounded the corner and nearly fell when her foot slipped on flour on the floor. Actually, there was flour everywhere. And splatters of...well, she wasn't sure what the reddish brown stuff was on the cabinets and counters. She did recognize the linguini noodles stuck to the wall, though.

She wasn't going to ask.

Wraith, looking unexpectedly sexy in jeans, no shirt, and an apron, turned away from a pot of boiling water to toss a fork into the pile of pots and pans in the sink. He must have used every dish in the house.

"Way. And this morning I learned to tie my shoes."

She laughed, relieved to find that their little spat hadn't made things weird. Maybe talking about it would be easier than she'd even hoped for.

"Both feats are impressive," she teased. "Now if you can master peanut butter and jelly sandwiches for Stew I'd be *really* impressed."

"Peanut butter sticks to the bread and rips it apart. It's stupid. I need to introduce Stewie to bologna sandwiches. Those things kept me alive for a year once. No joke."

He shot her one of his patented you-gotta-love-me smiles and pulled a baking dish out of the oven. She moved closer to see what was in the dish and was shocked to see oysters swimming in butter. She loved them, but Wraith wasn't a fan...something about how they looked like they'd come from out of a harpies' nose.

And yet, he ate Spam.

"Speaking of Stewie, where is he?"

He dumped the boiling pot into a strainer in the sink, and linguini plopped out. Explained the noodles on the wall. Sort of. "He's in bed."

"Did you feed him dinner first?"

"You ask me that a lot."

"Because of the time you forgot to feed him."

"Ah, that. Well, he can talk now. He doesn't let me forget." He smiled at her, his lips softening as he went from flirty amusement to genuine happiness. "I'm glad you're home."

"I am too." She nodded at the stove, where a covered pot seemed on the verge of boiling over. "Do you need some help?"

"Nope. It's done. If you want to pour the wine, we can eat."

"You got it." While she poured the merlot he'd opened and set out to breathe, he finished up and loaded the table with food.

"I made grilled oysters," he said, a little sheepishly, "but I made them too early and had to put them in the oven to stay warm." He shrugged. "I'd say I might have ruined them, but they're floofing oysters. How the hell would you know they're ruined?"

She punched him lightly in the shoulder, and he grinned. "What? They're nasty. But they're supposed to be aphrodisiacs, and I figured that after my bullshit, I needed all the help I could get with you tonight. I even got the recipes from one of Suzanne's romance-themed shows. See?" He gestured with a serving spoon at the laptop on the counter, which was streaming an episode of *Angel in the Kitchen*. "She showed me how to make Seafood Linguini."

The amount of effort he'd gone to made her heart clench. Wraith showed her all the time how much he loved her, but he'd always done it in ways that were unique to him and in ways he excelled. He definitely didn't excel at cooking, so seeing him go to this kind of effort filled her with both joy and guilt.

"Oh, Wraith, I'm so sorry I freaked out like that. I think I took what you said the wrong way because *I* was the one who was afraid you felt that way. I've been feeling kind of insecure lately."

"Why?"

She sank down in the chair and waited for Wraith to do the same.

"I'm really freaking about how Stew will react when we tell him the truth about his birth. We have to do it soon. He's far from stupid. He figured out on his own that Mace was his brother -- it's only a matter of time before he learns that vampires can't give birth."

"That's not entirely true..."

She gave him a *get serious* look. "Your circumstances were unique." And bizarre. Sometimes she was amazed that there weren't more bats in Wraith's belfry.

"He'll be fine," Wraith said as he presented her with an oyster in a cute little leaf dish. "He knows all about our species. He knows how we reproduce. Most Sems are killed at birth or have shitty mothers, 'cause, you know, demons. We never even meet our fathers. It won't matter to Stewie that you didn't give birth to him. You *are* his mother. It'll be okay."

She wanted to believe that. She was *desperate* to believe that. "But what if it's not? Most Sems are raised in Sheoul. They grow up among demons. But you've got humans in the mix now, and this will be the first generation of Sems who are growing up in truly a human society, with human family traditions and customs. I mean, he even goes by Stewie instead of his given name." Her hand trembled as she picked up the oyster dish. "We need to tell him the truth, Wraith," she whispered. "But I'm afraid."

"Mama?"

Startled, Serena dropped her oyster and they both whipped around in their seats. Stewie stood at the entrance to the kitchen, his favorite blanket wrapped around his shoulders, his Spiderman pajamas hanging loosely on his little body.

"Stewie," she gasped. "Honey, what are you doing?"

He tugged the blanket more tightly around him. "I wanted a drink of water and I heard you talking."

Oh, no.

"Hey, buddy." Wraith stood. "Let's get you some water and get you back to bed."

"But Mama's afraid."

Her heart cracked right down the middle. "Oh, baby, I'm perfectly safe. We all are."

He looked down at his bare feet. "You're afraid of telling me the truth. I heard you."

Closing her eyes, she swallowed hard, trying to keep tears from forming.

"We can talk about this later," Wraith said.

"But I wanna make Mommy feel better."

Serena threw her arms wide. "Give me a hug. That'll make it all better."

Stewie ran over and threw himself into her lap. He smelled like bubblegum soap and blue raspberry shampoo. Wraith had even remembered to make him take a bath.

"I know vampires can't have babies," he said, his big brown eyes locking onto hers, wise beyond their years. She'd always told Wraith that he had an ancient soul, and times like these confirmed it.

"So you know…" She didn't know how to say it. She'd been preparing for this moment for seven years, and she still wasn't ready.

"I know I was in someone else's belly." Stewie yawned and rubbed his lids. "Am I like Mace? Is someone like Aunt Tayla my secret other mother?"

Serena hugged Stewie close. "No, sweetheart." She pressed a kiss into his silky hair. "Is that why you've been angry lately? You thought your birth mother was part of your life and we didn't tell you?"

He nodded and looked over at Wraith. "Who was she? My other mother."

Wraith paled. For all his assurances that Stewie would be fine with the information, he was worried, too. "This is something we'll talk about when you're older, kiddo. All you need to know right now is that we love you and that your mother, your *real* mother, is the one who has been there for you since the day you were born."

"I know." Stewie looked up at Serena. "You will always be my mama. I'm glad it was you."

Her heart swelled until it felt like it might burst. "I'm glad it was me too. I can't imagine my life without you."

Stewie smiled and then sniffed the air. "What are you eating?"

She glanced over at Wraith. "We were enjoying a romantic dinner."

Wraith nodded, a mutual understanding building between them. "But you know what, buddy? Let's make it a family dinner. There's nothing more important than that." Wraith lowered his voice to a conspiratorial stage whisper. "Besides, you know you want to stick around to try my grilled harpy boog--"

"*Wraith!*"

Wraith watched as Stewie and Serena finished the last of the Red Devil's Food Cake. Stew had managed to get frosting all over his face, but it was adorable. Serena hadn't gotten even a smudge on her lips, but Wraith had set aside a little frosting for...later. Oh, yeah, she was going to get frosting all over, and he planned to get it all over *his* face when he licked it off of her.

Dinner had been fun. No, he hadn't planned on it being a family affair... he'd wanted to seduce Serena with every bite, to feed her oysters with his own hand and then play Lady and the Tramp with the linguini. But the bonding they'd done as a family had been even better.

Wraith had grown up without love. His father had been absent, but the guy had been a monster, so that was no loss. His mother had tortured him and kept him in a cage. But eventually he'd escaped and had been found by his brothers, who had taught him what family was.

It was because of Shade and Eidolon that Wraith had been able to accept Serena into his life, and it was because of Serena that he could be a father.

So, no, she hadn't given birth to Stewie, but she'd still made him a dad.

Shade liked to say that life often threw curve balls.

Pretty cool that Wraith had finally learned to catch them.

Wraith, along with his brothers Eidolon and Shade, are the foundation characters on which my Demonica series was based. Wraith plays a prominent role in *Pleasure Unbound* and *Desire Unchained*, books 1 and 2 of the Demonica series, and he finds his mate, Serena, in book 3, *Passion Unleashed,* so if you're curious about the origins of the family you just read about, any of those books will be a good place to start. Enjoy!

ROMANTIC/SEXY FOOD

Grilled Oysters with Spicy Butter

1 cup (2 sticks) butter

1 lemon, juiced

¼ cup minced garlic

¼ cup fresh horseradish

1 teaspoon salt

1 teaspoon pepper

2 dozen fresh oysters

½ cup chopped chives

In a small saucepan over low heat, add the butter, lemon juice, garlic, horseradish, salt and pepper and stir until melted. Remove from heat. Shuck the oysters and spoon 1 teaspoon of sauce in each oyster. Place oysters on direct heat of a preheated 400 degree grill, cover and cook for 5-6 minutes or until the edges of oysters curl slightly. Remove from grill and top with chives and more sauce if desired.

Quick Tip: If you are unable to shuck oysters because they are tightly closed, simply place them on the preheated grill and close lid for 1 minute. Remove with an oven mitt and shuck. The short time on the grill will allow them to open slightly so that a shucking knife is easy to use.

Seafood Linguine

1 (16 ounce) box linguine

½ cup olive oil

8 tablespoons (1 stick) butter

1 onion, diced

2 tablespoons minced garlic

1 cup dry white wine

1 (28 ounce) can San Marzano tomatoes, pureed

1 teaspoon dried basil

1 teaspoon dried oregano

¼ teaspoon salt

¼ teaspoon pepper

1 pound (21-30) count shrimp, peeled and deveined

½ pound sea scallops

½ pound lump crabmeat

1 bunch parsley, chopped, for garnish

Cook linguine per package directions. In a large skillet, over medium heat, add oil, butter, onion, and garlic. Cook until onions are translucent and softened, about 3-5 minutes. Add the wine and stir until liquid has evaporated. Reduce heat to low and add in tomatoes, basil, oregano, salt and pepper. Allow to simmer for 10-15 minutes. Add the seafood and continue to simmer for an additional 5 minutes, or until shrimp are pink. Serve over cooked linguine and garnish with parsley.

Stuffed Flank Steak

2 pounds flank steak, butterflied

3 tablespoons panko breadcrumbs

2 cups shredded mozzarella cheese

1 cup frozen spinach, thawed and drained

½ cup sun-dried tomatoes, chopped

1 teaspoon minced garlic

¼ teaspoon salt

¼ teaspoon pepper

2 tablespoons olive oil

Preheat oven to 425 degrees. Place the steak on a cutting board and cover the top with plastic wrap. Using a rolling pin or meat mallet, pound meat to an even ½ inch thickness. In a large bowl, mix together remaining ingredients except for olive oil. Spread mixture over the entire surface of flank steak. Roll the steak up into a pinwheel and tie with butcher's twine in 4 places down the length of the steak. Place in a 9 x 13-inch baking dish and rub the entire surface with olive oil. Add additional salt and pepper to the outside. Bake for 40 minutes, then turn on broiler and cook for an additional 5 minutes. Remove from oven and let rest for 10 minutes before slicing.

Red Devil's Food Cake

1 box Devil's Food Cake

1 cup buttermilk

½ cup oil

3 eggs

1 (1 ounce) bottle red food coloring

Chocolate Icing

Cream Cheese Icing

Preheat oven to 350 degrees. In a large bowl, using a hand mixer, beat together the cake mix, buttermilk, oil, eggs and food coloring until blended. Pour into three greased 9-inch cake pans. Bake for 20-25 minutes or until toothpick inserted in the center comes out clean. Remove from oven and cool for 10 minutes. Remove from cake pans and allow to cool completely on a cooling rack. While the cakes are cooling, prepare the icing. When the cakes are cooled, spread a thin layer of Chocolate Icing on 2 of the cake layers. Using a piping bag, pipe the Cream Cheese Icing on top of the Chocolate Icing. Stack the cake starting with the 2 chocolate layers and ending with the third. Ice the cake on all sides with the Cream Cheese Icing and smooth with a knife.

Cream Cheese Icing

8 tablespoons (1 stick) butter, softened

1 (8 ounce) block cream cheese, softened

1 teaspoon vanilla extract

3 cups confectioner's sugar

In a large bowl, using a hand mixer, combine butter, cream cheese, and vanilla until blended. Add powdered sugar one cup at a time until all 3 cups are blended.

Chocolate Icing

1 stick butter, softened

⅔ cup cocoa powder

3 cups powdered sugar

⅓ cup milk

1 teaspoon vanilla extract

Melt butter in a microwave safe bowl for 1 minute. Stir in cocoa. Add powdered sugar, milk and vanilla, mixing to a spreading consistency. Add small amount of additional milk, if needed.

Steak Bruschetta with Onion Jam

1 sirloin steak (1-2 pounds)

1 tablespoon Montreal steak seasoning

½ cup balsamic vinegar

1 cup extra virgin olive oil

1 tablespoon minced garlic

1 French loaf

2 cups Onion Jam

1 cup crumbled blue cheese

Salt and pepper

Preheat oven to 400 degrees. Season the steak with steak seasoning and grill on medium heat until cooked to your preference. Set steak aside to rest. In a small bowl, combine the vinegar, oil and garlic together. Slice the French loaf in half lengthwise and brush half of the oil mixture onto each side of the bread. Place the bread on a cookie sheet and bake for 5 minutes. While the bread is baking, slice the steak very thinly. Remove bread from oven and layer the thinly sliced steak onto your bread. Top with Onion Jam, blue cheese and about half of the remaining oil mixture. Return to the oven for an additional 2-3 minutes. Slice loaf halves into 2 inch thick pieces and serve with remaining sauce for dipping.

Onion Jam

¼ cup oil

3 large sweet onions, thinly sliced

¾ cup sugar

½ cup apple cider vinegar

In a large skillet, over medium heat, add the oil and onions and cook, stirring occasionally for 15-20 minutes, or until golden brown. Reduce heat to low and sprinkle sugar over onions. Add in vinegar and continue to cook for an additional 10 minutes, stirring occasionally. Serve immediately or place in Mason jars for future use. It will keep for 6 weeks refrigerated.

Bananas Foster Crème Brulee

2 cups heavy cream

½ cup sugar

1 tablespoon vanilla extract

5 egg yolks

Preheat oven to 275. In a medium bowl, using a hand mixer, combine the cream, sugar, vanilla and egg yolks. Add to 6 greased ramekins and place in a large pan filled with 1 inch of water. Bake for 60 minutes and remove from oven. Instead of adding sugar to torch, the Bananas Foster will be added.

Bananas Foster

3 tablespoons butter

3 tablespoons brown sugar

3 bananas, sliced in small rounds

3 tablespoons hazelnut liqueur (or rum)

6 teaspoons white sugar

In a large skillet over medium heat, melt the butter and brown sugar. Add bananas and turn the heat up to high. Add the hazelnut liqueur. Shake the pan a little bit, then flip each banana. Once the liqueur has reduced, turn off the heat. Arrange the bananas over the custard and sprinkle with a teaspoon of white sugar. Use a torch to burn the top and get a caramelized topping.

Caprese Chicken with Balsamic Glaze

4 boneless, skinless chicken breasts

¼ teaspoon salt

¼ teaspoon pepper

1 teaspoon dried basil

1 teaspoon dried oregano

2 Roma tomatoes, sliced

1 ball fresh mozzarella cheese, sliced

8 fresh basil leaves

1 tablespoon olive oil

2 tablespoons minced garlic

½ cup balsamic vinegar

2 tablespoons dark brown sugar

Preheat oven to 350 degrees. Cut a pocket about 3/4 of the way through on the thickest side of each breast, being careful not to cut all the way. Season chicken with salt, pepper, dried basil and dried oregano. Fill each pocket with 2 slices fresh tomato, 1 slice mozzarella cheese and 2 basil leaves. Seal with 3-4 toothpicks diagonally to keep the filling inside during cooking. In a large skillet over medium-high heat, heat a tablespoon of oil, then add the chicken and cook for 2 minutes on each side until golden. While the chicken is cooking, mix together the garlic, balsamic vinegar and brown sugar in a small bowl. Pour the mixture into the pan around the chicken; bring to a simmer, stirring occasionally, until the glaze has slightly thickened (about 2-3 minutes). Place pan in the oven and

continue to cook for 10-15 minutes, or until the chicken is cooked through and the cheese has melted. Remove toothpicks before serving.

*They have hot peppers in Louisiana. Little red devils
with fire in their skin and hell in their seeds.*
~James Street, "The Grains of Paradise"

HARVESTER *and* REAVER

Dark Chocolate Chipotle Brownies

Grilled Beef Skewers with Wasabi Aioli

White Chicken Chili

Gumbo

Zesty Lemon Mahi Mahi

Salsa with a Vengeance

Spicy Sticky Ribs

HARVESTER AND REAVER

"I can't believe we're going to be on TV." Harvester, whose given angelic name was actually Verrine, grinned at Reaver as they waited for their cue to join Suzanne on the set of her cooking show, Angel in the Kitchen.

"I can't either," he muttered. "The producers of this show must be insane."

Harvester blinked at him, but her wide-eyed innocence was as fake as the fruit in the bowl next to them. "I don't know what you mean."

She knew exactly what he meant, but he played her game and explained. "Viewers think the people on this show are human actors playing characters. So if one of us, for example, *you*, goes off script, it could put not just the show, but all of Heaven's carefully laid plans, in jeopardy."

"You worry too much." She reached up and gave him a playful love tap on the nose. "You're so not the angel I fell in love with all those thousands of years ago."

"Is that a bad thing?"

Her voice went low and smoky, a tone she usually reserved for the bedroom. Or for when they were in public and he couldn't do anything about the arousal she stirred up in him.

"Oh, no," she purred. "I love what you turned into even more."

They'd had a long, hard road to get to where they were, but every agony they'd been through had been worth it. And there had been a lot of agony, some of it at each others' hands.

Most of it, actually. Like back when she was evil and she'd collapsed a mountain on top of him. Or the time she'd kept him chained and drugged after sawing off his wings. Or when he'd tried to kill her once or a dozen times. But really, who was counting?

A lighted sign came on, indicating that filming was about to commence. Everyone hushed as Suzanne greeted the audience and introduced her first guest, Harvester.

This was going to be interesting. The hold-your-breath-in-anticipation-of-disaster kind of interesting.

Harvester, dressed in a sleek black pantsuit with a peek-a-boo red bra and matching high heels, strode onto the kitchen set, and after a little introductory banter, she and Suzanne settled into the business of cooking.

"So, before we get started," Suzanne said, "I'd like to ask about your own background in the kitchen."

Harvester smiled. "I don't have much. My mate does most of the cooking. Honestly, I don't even understand that. We can eat out anywhere in the world, after all. Why spend time in the kitchen?"

"So you aren't one for a personal touch, then?"

"Oh, don't misunderstand me," Harvester said brightly. "I've made revenge food. That's very personal."

Suzanne's eyes narrowed. "Is that why you asked for this episode to feature spicy food?"

Harvester's smile turned as black as her hair. She might be a fully-restored Heavenly angel, but eons spent in hell had given her a wicked sense of humor. "Absolutely."

"Well, we can do that." Suzanne turned to the camera. "Today we're going to spice up your life with a little sweet, a little salty, and a whole lot of spicy."

Reaver stood back, watching as Suzanne and Harvester prepared dark chocolate chipotle brownies. Harvester wanted to add more spice in the form of Diablo Claw peppers from one of Sheoul's arid agricultural regions, but Suzanne insisted that underworlders could make the substitution in their own kitchens. Which sounded reasonable, given that when cooked, the gas released by Diablo Claw peppers could melt human eyeballs, and several crew members wouldn't appreciated being blinded by brownies.

After the brownies came out of the oven, Harvester tasted one and moaned. "It's incredible. Reminds me of a dessert I had in New Orleans once."

"I love New Orleans. There's so much great food there. So," Suzanne said, "what's your opinion of beignets?"

"Bidets?" Harvester reached for the glass of wine Suzanne had poured a few minutes earlier. "Life changing."

Suzanne laughed. "No, not bidets. Beignets."

"Oh. Well, I like those too. But bidets? So refreshing."

"Yes, I'm sure--"

"And after sex?" Harvester made a sound of pure pleasure, familiar enough to Reaver to make him wish they were near a bed. Or a wall. Or... well, anything would do. "Oh. My. God. Like I said, life changing."

"I...ah..." Suzanne swallowed, clearly flustered. "I don't think bidets are exactly a cooking show topic..."

"Hmph. Then they shouldn't make 'em so great. And seriously, bidets are a forbidden subject? You've had demons on your show." Harvester shrugged. "But sure, you wanted to talk about beignets?"

Suzanne breathed a sigh of relief. "Yes, please."

"Little pillows of fried dough?" Harvester made another, smaller, moan of pleasure. "You eat enough of those and you'll be happy you have a bidet, let me tell you."

Delicate blooms of pink colored Suzanne's cheeks, and the mischievous twinkle in Harvester's eyes had Reaver deciding it was time to rescue poor Suzanne. He signaled to the producer, who nodded vehemently.

He joined Suzanne and Harvester, and fortunately, the talk turned almost exclusively to food, and by the time the show was over, he'd gotten his fill of brownies, Spicy Sticky Ribs, and something called Salsa with a Vengeance, which Harvester thought needed a lot more "vengeance." The Diablo Claw peppers came up again, and naturally, so did bidets.

Ah, well. Inappropriateness was part of Harvester's charm. She certainly kept things interesting, which she proved when the show ended and she dragged him into the green room for some post-taping fun.

It was only as they were readjusting their clothes that a sudden suspicion came over him. He couldn't even say why. Harvester wasn't behaving strangely at all. And maybe that was the problem. She'd actually been on her best behavior for days.

"Is everything okay?" he asked as he unlocked the green room door.

She frowned. "Of course. Why?"

"Because you're being extra normal."

Her eyes shot wide in mock horror. "Oh, no. Maybe I should see a doctor."

"I wouldn't put any doctor through that. Not even Eidolon." He actually considered the demon doctor and his ex-employer to be one of his best friends, but it was fun to torment the guy now and then. "Seriously...is there anything you want to talk about?"

"As a matter of fact, there is," she said. "We need to discuss a baby shower gift for Cara and Ares."

Yes, they did. But shopping for the perfect present wasn't the topic that was scratching at the edges of his angelic intuition. On the other hand, Harvester wasn't going to open up until she was ready, so for now he let it go.

Still, something told him he'd better buckle up and hold on to his halo.

———◆◆◆◆◆———

Harvester glanced at Reaver as they materialized inside their Heavenly palace. His face was still flushed from the sex in the green room, and he looked as handsome as ever in fitted black slacks and a sapphire shirt that matched his eyes. His shoulder-length golden hair, which she'd tousled with her fingers, was silky smooth again, making her itch with the desire to muss it up. She liked it when her perfect angel was a little rough around the edges. A little dirty, even.

"I really think that went well," she said as she tossed her shoulder bag onto the couch.

"Any time you don't destroy a building or kill someone, I consider it having gone well."

She snorted. "I'm not that bad."

"You've gotten better," he conceded. "You haven't killed another angel in months."

"See? Progress." She went up on her toes and gave him a playful kiss, getting him ready for the topic she was about to bring up. She hadn't wanted to talk to him yet, but damn him, he could read her like an ancient text from the Akashic Library. "What do you say I pour a couple glasses of Champagne and we hop in the hot spring?"

Their luxurious tub, carved from crystal and fed by a natural effervescent spring, overlooked the majestic Blue Mountains of Trinity in the distance. During her time as a fallen angel Harvester had spent thousands of years in the ugly gloom of hell, and now she took every opportunity to soak in the magnificence of Heaven.

Reaver frowned. "Did you forget? We're supposed to be at Reseph and Jillian's place in five minutes."

Shit. She'd totally forgotten. Or maybe she'd blocked it out. "Why did we agree to go again?"

"Because Jillian said there's something weird going on with her bond with Tracker."

Oh, right. She vaguely remembered Reaver telling her the slave bond Harvester had transferred to Jillian had been acting up. The bond connecting Jillian to a werewolf named Tracker wasn't meant to be hosted by humans, so it wasn't surprising that Jillian would experience glitches.

"Damn," she sighed.

Reaver caught her by the arm. "Hey, seriously. What is it? Something to do with Reseph?"

Bingo. She just hated discussing the Four Horsemen with Reaver. He always took their sides over hers, and as their father, he was a little overprotective and blind to their faults. Maybe because he hadn't even known they were his children until recently, and guilt probably played a role in his feelings toward them.

"It's just..." She squared her shoulders and spit it out. "I have a feeling he's going to do something stupid."

Reaver cocked a skeptical eyebrow. "You say that all the time."

Yeah, she did.

But this was different.

"This isn't my Watcher spidey-sense. And it isn't my wicked stepmonster bias." She loved the Horsemen, but that hadn't always been the case. And while she did love them, she didn't always like them.

And the feeling was generally mutual. Her relationship with Reseph was particularly complex given that, after Reseph's Seal had broken and he'd become the evil being known as Pestilence, he'd tortured and abused her like none ever had. Not in her thousands of years of being an angel, and then a fallen angel, and now an angel again.

"Okay, so what do you think he's going to do?" Reaver folded his arms over his chest as he shifted into his overprotective father mode. "Something you'll get to punish him for?"

"I can only hope," she said, joking. Mostly. "But I have no idea. Like I said, it's just a sense I get."

"Well," he said, taking her hand. "Let's see if we can figure it out. Just try not to antagonize him."

"Me? Pfft. Never."

He ignored that, and a heartbeat later, they were standing at the door to Jillian and Reseph's Colorado cabin, where Jillian met them with a smile and mimosas. Ah, the human female knew Harvester so well.

"Thanks for coming," Jillian said as she closed the door. She was wearing jeans and a light green sweater, perfect attire for the chilly fall weather. Her dark bob just brushed her shoulders, pulled up in a clip on one side. She was adorable, smart, and sensitive; the exact opposite of the skanky females Reseph had sleazed around with in the past.

Jillian was the best thing that had ever happened to Reseph, and Harvester swore that if he screwed things up with his mate, Harvester would fry him with a Heavenly tempest that would take decades to recover from.

"Hey." Reseph strode out of the bedroom, his big body encased in armor, his white-blond hair tied back with a leather thong at the nape of his neck. "Wish I could stay, but I have to go."

"Is it something I did?" Harvester asked innocently.

Reseph's blue eyes, usually sparkling with mischief and humor, shifted to her, bloodshot and swimming with shadows. Before Harvester became the Horsemen's Heavenly Watcher, she'd been their evil Sheoulic Watcher, and she recognized that look. A plague somewhere on the planet was drawing him so intensely that it hurt. He could only resist for so long, and if he was armored, he was on his way to the outbreak.

His voice rumbled, thick and raspy with exhaustion and pain. "What, you think I need to go just because you cursed me with Khileshi cockfire last month?"

Hilarity. Pure hilarity. "You're just lucky I didn't opt for the extra ooze upgrade."

"Well, why the hell not?" He drew his sword from the scabbard at his hip to test the edge. "Boils and burning flesh that peeled like a flambéed banana wasn't enough?"

Harvester took a sip of her mimosa. "I do adore Jillian. I didn't want to distress her too much."

Reseph gaped. "Distress *Jillian*?"

"Ahem." Reaver's voice was mild and pleasant. Which meant he was reining in his annoyance. Yeah, well, when he interfered in her Watcher business, *she* had to rein in *her* annoyance. "You gave him a demonic venereal disease?"

"Oh, chill out," she sighed. "It was Watcher punishment. And it was pathetically mild. I mean, how long did it take to run its course? Twelve hours?"

"Fifteen. And a half. And my piss burned like acid for three days afterward," Reseph grumbled as he shoved the sword back into the scabbard.

He swung around to Jillian, and his tone softened. "I gotta go, Jilly." He pulled her into his arms and kissed her long enough to make Harvester and Reaver turn away. "I'll miss you."

With that, he stalked outside and threw open a gate to wherever he was going.

"There's a plague in China," Jillian explained. "He's been resisting the call to go, but we both knew he couldn't wait another day, let alone another hour."

As the Horseman associated with disease and pestilence, Reseph was drawn to outbreaks, just as his sister Limos was drawn to famine, Ares was drawn to war, and Thanatos was drawn to death. Poor Thanatos had it the worst of all of them, since death was the result of disease, famine, and war, so he often haunted the same scenes as his siblings.

"I didn't know about this plague," Reaver said to Harvester. "I'm going to check it out while you two do whatever you need to do. I'll meet you at our new condo." He flashed out of the house, leaving Harvester with Jillian.

"I *am* sorry about the Khileshi cockfire," Harvester said. "Well, I'm sorry for you. Reseph deserved it."

Jillian eyed her skeptically. "Did he?"

Harvester shrugged. "He slaughtered a demon who was under Memitim protection. Truly, I went easy on him." She took another sip of her mimosa. "Now, let's take care of your problem. What's happening with the bond?"

"I used to be able to feel when Tracker was in pain." Jillian glanced out the window at the small cabin she and Reseph had built as a residence for the werewolf. "But during the last full moon when he shifted, he got into a battle with some other werewolves and he nearly bled to death. I didn't feel a thing."

"Huh." Harvester put down the glass and pressed her palm against Jillian's breastbone. Closing her eyes, she let herself feel for the energy signature that was unique to both Jillian and Tracker, and once she found it, she discovered that one of the "tethers," as she called them, had frayed. With a punch of energy, she repaired the thread. "There. It's fixed. Let me know if this happens again."

"Are you sure the bond can't be destroyed?"

"We've been over this," Harvester reminded her. "The bond is part of Tracker. Destroying it will kill him. It can only be transferred. Do you have someone you want to transfer it to?"

"No." Jillian glanced out the window again. Tracker was out there now, raking leaves. He was never idle, a trait beaten into all bond-slaves from infancy. "I just want him to be happy."

"Are you?"

Jillian blinked, taken aback. "What? Happy? With Tracker?"

"With everything."

Something in Jillian's expression triggered Harvester's alarm bells, but it was gone as fast as it came. "I'm very happy."

"I see."

"You don't believe me?" Jillian sank down on the couch, annoying her cat, Doodle, who reached out to swat her before curling up again.

Harvester wasn't sure how to answer. She knew Reseph and Jillian were happy with each other, but something told her a big change was in the wind. She couldn't tell if it was going to be a good change or a bad one, but she had no doubt it could be traced back to her sense that Reseph was going to do something dumb.

"I don't have any reason not to believe you," Harvester hedged. "But if there's anything you ever want to discuss, I have a willing ear."

"I appreciate that." Jillian patted the chair next to the couch. "Now, tell me about Suzanne's show. Was it fun being a guest?"

Harvester laughed as she sat down. "Absolutely. But I doubt Suzanne will invite me back."

Jillian smirked, a reliable sister in mischief. "What did you do?"

"Me?" Harvester smiled into her champagne flute. "Nothing. She's the one with silly rules. Can you believe you're not supposed to talk about bidets on a cooking show?"

"You didn't."

"Oh, please," Harvester said with a dismissive wave. "You can talk about food going in but not coming out? In any case, she's sparked my interest in cooking. I think I'll give it a shot. I'm going to make some homemade treats for Cara's hellhounds, too. I'm becoming quite domestic."

Jillian clearly wasn't buying it, but then, being mated to Reseph had given her a lot of practice sifting through bullshit.

"Well, if you need some easy recipes, let me know. Reseph would rather eat hearty meals at home than go out, so I do a lot of cooking."

"Does Reseph cook?"

"Actually, he does. He grills a lot, and he bought a smoker a few weeks back. We now have enough smoked meats in the freezer to feed Ares for a year." Smiling, Jillian toyed with Doodle's paws. "He actually wanted to give some ham and sausages to Cara as a baby shower gift."

"I doubt Ares would complain. He eats more than a dozen men can eat at a sitting."

Jillian nodded absently, her gaze turned inward, and Harvester frowned. There was something bothering the other female, but Harvester wasn't sure if she should press more. She wasn't very good at coaxing information from people. Her style was more along the lines of torturing or, at the very least, annoying her target until they talked, but obviously, that wasn't an option.

Cautiously, she dipped a toe in. "Are you sure there's nothing wrong? Nothing you want to talk about?"

"I'm sure," Jillian said, a little too cheerily. "But you know what I'd like to do?"

"What's that?"

"Shop. If you're not busy, want to go do a little baby shower shopping in Paris?"

Harvester grinned. She wasn't much into girl stuff, but she loved going to hoity-toity, upscale shops and floofing with snotty employees and haughty, self-important customers.

What a perfect ending to a perfect day.

Reaver hated plagues. The stench of sickness and death burned the nose, and the sights and sounds of human suffering couldn't be wiped from memory.

He wished he could interfere -- and he could, if the plague was of demonic origin. But no, this was an old-fashioned viral hemorrhagic fever originally caused by an animal bite. Not long ago, he might have snapped his fingers and ended it, but now that he was privy to what he called the Universal Plan, he understood why these things happened.

And needed to happen.

But that didn't change the fact that the human realm could be an awful place.

A wave of power engulfed him from behind, spiderwebbing across his skin in streaks of electricity. He didn't have to look to know an archangel had just paid him a visit.

"Yenrieth."

Grateful for a distraction, he turned away from the tragic scene in the village below. "'Sup, Mike." Reaver flared his gold wings, a reminder that he outranked and outgunned the archangel by a factor of about a thousand. "And it's Reaver. Not Yenrieth."

"Yeah, well, it's Michael, not Mike."

Mike seemed testy today. "Now that we're clear on names," Reaver drawled, "wanna tell me why you're here?"

The archangel growled deep in his chest. "I still don't know how it came to be that you were raised to Radiant status."

Yes, he did. He was just being an ass. "I could remind you, but we both know you're too envious to care."

All angels were envious that Reaver, who had once been punished with expulsion from Heaven and centuries of memory loss, had been awarded the status of the Radiant. Only one Radiant existed at a time, more powerful than all the archangels put together, and there wasn't an angel, fallen or not, in Heaven or Sheoul, who believed he deserved the position.

Reaver didn't really believe it either, but who was he to question the Almighty? Besides, it was floofing awesome being at the very top of the food chain. So he rolled with it. Times like this, when he had to deal with angels who had once treated him like dirt, he reveled in it.

Michael exhaled in a huff. "You're...exasperating."

"Harvester is rubbing off on me." At the sudden glint in Michael's eye, Reaver went taut. "That's why you're here. It's about Harvester."

Dipping his head in acknowledgment, the archangel clasped his hands in front of his purple and gold robes. "The Watcher Council has agreed to consider your request," he said. "I believe we'll vote to remove Harvester as the Horsemen's Watcher."

"What?" Reaver cursed. "I didn't ask you to remove her. I asked you find a replacement for her."

"How is that not asking us to fire her?"

"I just want her to have an option."

"Why?"

Because she hates the job.

She was always complaining about it, and in Reaver's opinion, she enjoyed taking out her frustration on the Horsemen. She wasn't harsh with them...in fact, Reaver had gone harder on them when he'd been their Watcher. But she was just...mean.

"It doesn't matter why."

"Then it won't matter if we replace her."

Reaver stepped closer, his wings flaring of their own accord. "Don't do it, Mikey. Not until I make sure it's what Harvester wants."

"You have twelve human hours to decide. If we don't hear from you, Harvester will be reassigned."

"No, you'll hear from *her*. This is her decision, not mine. Also," he said in a voice that resonated through the air like thunder, "you will not reassign her. The sacrifices she made for Heaven and mankind can't be overstated. She's earned the right to do any job she wants...or to not have a job at all. Is that understood?"

Michael might be an arrogant ass, but he wasn't stupid or petty, and he respected what Harvester had done to save the world. He nodded. "She deserves to be revered in every corner of the universe." His mouth quirked. "It would be nice if she made it easier to do."

Yeah, that was Harvester. Reaver had penetrated the layers of walls she'd put up, and many of them had come down. But those that remained were as tall and thick as ever, and few made it past them.

"Twelve hours, Radiant."

Michael shot upward in a flurry of wings and light, disappearing a split-second later.

What a weird ending to a weird day.

Reaver materialized in the living room of the Spanish condo he and Harvester had acquired a few months ago. Her goal was to have a house or apartment on every continent and eventually in every country. For her, there wasn't enough time to do and see everything she wanted, and seeing how she'd spent thousands of years in the hell realm of Sheoul, Reaver didn't argue with her frantic need to do it all. Even if she wanted to do it all at once.

He started to call out to her when he turned to find his son-in-law, Arik, sitting in Reaver's favorite recliner, his dark head bent over his phone. From the sounds coming from the device, it appeared he was playing Candy Crush.

"Hey, Pops," he said, not looking up. "Harvester's in the kitchen. She said I could wait."

"What's up?" Reaver took a seat across from Arik and then shouted to Harvester. "I'm in the living room with Arik."

Something clinked from the kitchen. "I'll be right there," she replied. "I just need to wash the penis off my hands!"

"Can you bring me a beer when you come out?" He looked at Arik. "Want one?"

Arik stared at him. "Aren't you even going to ask?"

Laughing, Reaver kicked his feet up on the glass coffee table. "I've been with Harvester long enough to know better."

Arik shook his head in dismay.

"You wanna ask?" Reaver said with a gesture toward the kitchen. "Go ahead."

As predicted, Arik, ever the warrior, couldn't resist the challenge. "Harvester? Did you say you have to wash the penis off your hands?"

"Yep."

"Um...why?"

There was another clink. "Do you want me to bring you a beer with penis juice on my hands?"

"No, I mean--"

Reaver gave him a "told you so" look and tried to keep a straight face.

Arik cleared his throat and tried again. The fool. "Why do you have penis, uh, juice, on your hands?"

"For Cara's hellhounds. Part of the baby shower gift."

"Penises?"

She poked her head around the corner. "You know how humans give those nasty dried bully sticks to their dogs? Those are dried penises. Hellhounds like 'em fresh."

"You're right," Arik grumbled to Reaver. "I shouldn't have asked."

"I can't believe you doubted me." Reaver popped his feet back down on the floor and addressed the reason Arik was here. "Is everything okay with Limos and Keilani?"

"Yeah, yeah, everything's great. I'm here on DART business. Sort of." He tucked his phone in his jacket pocket. "Rumor has it that Azagoth has shut down Sheoul-gra. Evil souls are starting to cause problems. I don't suppose you can maybe have a chat with him?'

This was news to Reaver, but then he and Harvester had been spending more time on the Other Side than in the human realm, and they'd missed a few messages. "I'll see what I can do."

That seemed to satisfy Arik. "So have you seen Revenant lately?"

Reaver's twin brother, Revenant, hadn't come around in months, but he had a good excuse. "Turns out that running Hell is a big job and it takes a lot of time."

"Huh. Who would have thought, right?"

Reaver opened his mouth to reply, but a sudden burst of curses and the sound of pots and pans crashing around the kitchen shut him up.

Standing, Arik reached up to rub the back of his neck. "This seems like my cue to go."

Reaver's too. "Need a ride?"

"If you're offering."

More curses came from the kitchen, and Reaver decided that delaying his chat with Harvester could wait a couple more minutes.

He took Arik by the shoulder and flashed him to the Hawaiian house he shared with Limos and their daughter, Keilani. The baby was sleeping in her playpen and Limos was napping on the couch next to it.

Reaver wasn't going to stay and wake anyone up, but he did remain there for a minute, just gazing upon the beauty of the little family. Limos was living her dream, and Reaver couldn't be happier.

"You can stay as long as you want," Arik whispered, but no, Reaver had to go.

Harvester might not admit it, but she needed him, and he would never not be there for her.

But as he dematerialized, he realized he might need to learn to dodge pans.

Food dripped from walls and cabinets, and the beautiful tiled floor was covered in sauce and overturned dishes. At least the kitchen smelled good.

"I can't do this!"

Harvester never cried, but she was so frustrated that she was on the verge. Reining in her desire to destroy more than she already had, she dialed Suzanne, who answered on the second ring.

"Hello?"

"It's Harvester. I need help."

"What can I do for you?"

"I can't cook. I just got done with the penises, and now I'm trying to make this dish from a recipe, but it sucks and I suck and I just want to order food and tell Reaver I cooked it."

Suzanne laughed softly. "It's okay. I can help you through it. What are you trying to make? Something with...penises? Is it a demon dish?"

"I'm making Coq au Vin and Baked Alaska."

Harvester heard Suzanne inhale sharply. "Honey, Coq au Vin doesn't use, um, those kind of cocks."

"I'm not using penises for...that. Ew. Gross. I have chicken."

"Oh, good." Suzanne sounded relieved, but she clearly hadn't considered the possibilities of using penises in revenge food. "But Coq au Vin and Baked Alaska are two very complicated dishes. Why don't I send you recipes that are a little more user-friendly? I can even talk you through them if you need me to."

Harvester hated admitting defeat, but she really wanted to do this. "I suppose that could work."

"Okay, what is the occasion? That'll help me find the perfect dishes."

"No occasion. It's just that in a couple of weeks we're going to have to spend an entire day with all his kids at a baby shower, and I think he worries about how we'll all get along." Mainly, he worried she'd cause trouble. "So I need to bank some credit."

On the other end of the line, Suzanne laughed. "I think my Beef Skewers with Wasabi Aioli and the Dark Chocolate Chipotle Brownies we made during your taping will be perfect. I'll text you the recipes in a few minutes."

"Perfect. Thank you."

Harvester hung up just as Reaver walked into the kitchen.

He stopped and looked around, his expression unreadable. "Were you attacked by a horde of demons? Or was this a temper tantrum?"

"It was demons," she said with a haughty sniff. "Big ones. At least a dozen."

"I see." A soft glow flashed around him, and instantly, the kitchen was clean and the pots and pans were stacked neatly in the sink.

"I'm sorry," she sighed. "I've been a little stressed."

"I know." He strode over to her and folded her into his arms. She loved it when he did that. She used to fight it, but now she knew that taking comfort and relying on someone wasn't a weakness. It was, in fact, almost a necessity for survival. "But I might be able to help."

"What do you mean?"

He inhaled deep in his chest, as if he had to brace himself for whatever he was about to say, and she stiffened. "I spoke with Michael. The Watcher Council has agreed to take you off Watcher duty."

She tore away from Reaver as explosive anger blasted through her, and she suddenly wished the pots and pans were within reach. "They what? You did *what*?"

"I just thought maybe you aren't happy doing the job." He casually put himself between her and the pile of cookware. "You always say you hate it, and you don't like the Horsemen anyway."

Her anger veered to hurt and confusion. "I…I…Why would you say that?"

"Why?" he asked, incredulous. "You laughed about cursing Reseph with a disease so painful that some demons amputate their own dicks. You enjoy punishing them."

"No, I don't." She held up her hand to stop him from arguing. "Well, maybe I enjoyed giving Reseph the STD…but come on, that was hilarious."

She let out a chuckle before clearing her throat and getting serious again. She truly didn't want Reaver, or his children, to think she hated them, and it was possible -- maybe -- that she'd been a little too hard on them.

"This might surprise you," she said softly, "but I don't like seeing the Horsemen suffer, especially if whatever they did to get into trouble was something I'd do myself. And it usually is. I never lie when I say I hate this job. The rules are stupid."

His brow furrowed in confusion. "Then why do you keep doing it?"

Why, indeed. She'd wondered the same thing. At first, she thought maybe it was out of jealousy that the Horsemen weren't hers. They should have been. Instead he'd knocked up a wretched succubus and ruined everything.

Later she'd realized that she hadn't felt the need to keep them close because she didn't like them, but because she loved them. She just had trouble admitting it.

"Harvester?" he prompted, his voice taking on a soothing tone that always took her down a few notches and encouraged her to tell him the truth. To open up.

Not her strong suit.

But he deserved it, so she closed her eyes and ripped her emotions wide open.

"Because I can't let someone else punish them." She opened her eyes, catching his surprised gaze. "I don't mete out even half the suffering another Watcher would. You know that. Historically, each Watcher tries to outdo the last. When I was the Horsemen's evil Watcher, I did try. And I succeeded." She'd been harsh and brutal, and at the time, she'd compartmentalized it and let it go. Now...now her actions sat on her chest like an anvil. "I had to because my life, and theirs, and the fate of the entire floofing world rested in my ability to maintain my cover and be the evilest bitch I could be. Now I can make it up to them." She snorted. "Except Reseph. I'm not done with him yet."

"So you don't hate them?"

"No. Not at all." She took Reaver's hand and drew him close. "Sometimes I resent it when you take their sides instead of mine, but I love them and would never force you to choose between my love and theirs. Besides," she said brightly, "eventually we'll have our own child, and you'll love it more than the Horsemen...and that'll be that." She booped him on the nose. "What do you say we forget that I tried to cook and we go out to eat?"

He stood there like he had been poleaxed. And she knew his poleaxed expression because she'd done it to him once, back when she was evil and he was extra annoying.

"You...want to have a baby?"

"Well, not now. But eventually...yes. I can't let that whore, Lilith, be the only mother to your children." She placed her hand on his chest, her pulse quickening to match his as it thudded against her palm. "And no, my jealousy is not truly the reason I want a child. It's you, Reaver. For the longest time I didn't think I had enough love in my heart for anything more than what we have. But I keep finding new things to love. My world is getting bigger, and I want my family to do the same."

Suddenly, she found herself in Reaver's arms, his strength crushing her to him in a powerful embrace. His magnificent wings wrapped around them both, creating a cocoon of safety and love.

"Me too." His gaze captured hers, holding her in this perfect moment. And when his warm, firm lips came down on hers, she was reminded that, without a doubt, that he held her heart too…for all eternity.

Reaver and Harvester are one of my favorite couples in the Demonica/Lords of Deliverance universe, and if you liked them too, you can read all about their romance in REAVER. If you want to go back to their roots, you'll have to go all the way back to the first book in the Demonica series, Pleasure Unbound, where Reaver is but a mention. But by book 3, Passion Unleashed, he plays an important role that continues to this day. You'll meet Harvester in the 1st book of the Lords of Deliverance series, Eternal Rider, which is also book 6 of the Demonica series. I know, it's confusing, but feel free to check out my printable book list, which will help with the reading order!

SPICY FOOD

Dark Chocolate Chipotle Brownies

½ cup butter, melted

1 cup sugar

2 eggs

1 teaspoon vanilla

⅓ cup cocoa powder

½ cup all-purpose flour

¼ teaspoon baking powder

½ teaspoon cinnamon

1 teaspoon chipotle powder

Preheat oven to 350. Grease an 8 x 8-inch pan. Combine butter, sugar, eggs and vanilla in a large bowl. Add in cocoa powder, flour, baking powder, cinnamon and chipotle powder. Pour and spread into greased pan. Bake for 25 minutes. Let cool for 10 minutes then cover with frosting.

Chocolate Icing

½ cup (1 stick) butter or margarine, softened

⅔ cup cocoa powder

3 cups confectioners' sugar

⅓ cup milk

1 teaspoon vanilla extract

Melt butter. Stir in cocoa. Add powdered sugar, milk and vanilla. Mix well until smooth. Add a small amount of additional milk, if needed.

Grilled Beef Skewers with Wasabi Aioli

1 lemon, juiced

1 teaspoon ground ginger

1 teaspoon onion powder

2 tablespoons soy sauce

1 teaspoon minced garlic

1 (6 ounce) container plain Greek yogurt

1 (1-2 pound) sirloin steak, cut into 1-inch cubes

In a large resealable bag, combine the lemon juice, ground ginger, onion powder, soy sauce, minced garlic and yogurt. Add the steak and allow to marinate for 24 hours. Heat grill to medium heat. Thread 5-6 pieces of steak onto a kebab skewer. Repeat until all steak is skewered. Place on the grill over direct heat and cook for 3-4 minutes on each side or until desired doneness. Serve with Wasabi Aioli.

Wasabi Aioli

½ cup mayonnaise

1 tablespoon lemon juice

2 teaspoons wasabi paste

1 teaspoon minced garlic

In a small bowl, combine mayonnaise, lemon juice, wasabi paste and minced garlic. Refrigerate for 24 hours.

White Chicken Chili

4 boneless, skinless chicken breasts

1 onion, diced

1 tablespoon minced garlic

48 ounces chicken broth

2 (15 ounce) cans Great Northern beans, drained and rinsed

2 (4 ounce) cans green chiles

2 teaspoons salt

1 teaspoon cumin

1 teaspoon oregano

1 teaspoon chili powder

½ teaspoon cayenne pepper

½ cup fresh cilantro, chopped

1 cup heavy cream

1 teaspoon pepper

Topping

Sour cream

Monterey Jack cheese

Pickled jalapenos

Tortilla Strips

In a slow cooker, add chicken breasts and top with remaining ingredients except heavy cream. Cook on high for 4 hours. Remove chicken from slow cooker and shred on a cutting board. Return the chicken to the slow cooker and add heavy cream. Cook on high for an additional 15 minutes. Serve with sour cream, Monterey Jack cheese, pickled jalapenos and Tortilla Strips.

Tortilla Strips

4 cups oil

8 corn tortillas

2 teaspoons salt

Heat oil to 350 degrees. Slice corn tortillas in half, then slice in ½ inch thick strips and add to oil. Fry for 1-2 minutes, then drain and sprinkle with salt.

Gumbo

1 cup oil

1 cup flour

1 onion, chopped

1 red bell pepper, chopped

2 celery stalks, chopped

1 tablespoon minced garlic

1 pound smoked sausage, sliced ½ inch thick

1 tablespoon Creole seasoning

6 cups chicken broth

1 rotisserie chicken, shredded

Heat oil in a Dutch oven over medium heat and whisk in flour. Continue whisking until the roux has cooked for 8 to 10 minutes and is a dark tan in color. Stir onion, bell pepper, celery, garlic and sausage into roux. Season with Creole seasoning and continue to stir. Pour in the chicken broth. Bring to a boil over high heat, then reduce heat to low and simmer, uncovered, for 1 hour, stirring occasionally. Stir in shredded chicken and simmer for one more hour.

Zesty Lemon Mahi Mahi

4 mahi mahi fillets

1 stick butter, melted

1 lemon, juiced

1 teaspoon salt

1 teaspoon pepper

1 teaspoon paprika

1 teaspoon red pepper flakes

1 tablespoon onion powder

1 tablespoon garlic powder

3 tablespoons capers

Preheat oven to 350 degrees. In a 9 x 13-inch greased baking dish, lay the fillets out in a single layer. In a small bowl, whisk together the remaining ingredients and pour sauce evenly over the fillets. Bake for 25 minutes. Serve with additional sauce over fillets.

Quick Tip: Parchment paper is great for cooking fish. Place one fillet with 2-3 tablespoons of sauce in the center of a 12 inch piece of parchment paper. Pull paper over the fillet and fold to seal around the entire fish. This creates a steam oven. Bake for 20 minutes.

Salsa with a Vengeance

12 ripe tomatoes, quartered

1 (15 ounce) can san Marzano tomatoes

2 onions, quartered

¼ cup minced garlic

6 jalapenos, quartered

1 bunch fresh cilantro

3 limes, juiced

3 tablespoons ground cumin

2 tablespoons sugar

1 tablespoon salt

In a food processor, add tomatoes and pulse until pureed. Remove from food processor and place in a large bowl. Add remaining ingredients to the food processor and pulse until pureed. Add ingredients to the tomatoes and stir until blended together. Ladle salsa into 6 pint jars and seal. Follow directions below for canning to complete the process.

To prep the jars for canning, fill a large pot half-way with water. Place jars in water with lids removed. Bring to a boil over medium heat for 8-10 minutes. Remove and dry until ready for use. You may also use a dishwasher to wash and heat jars. After the jars have been filled with salsa, place the lids securely on each jar. Bring a large pot of water about ½ full to a rolling boil. Add the jars (about 6 pint or 10 jelly jars) to the pot, ensuring they are submerged. Boil for 10 minutes then remove from heat. Allow jars to stand for 10 minutes before removing from pot. Remove jars and allow to cool for 24 hours. Store in a cool dark place for up to a year.

Spicy Sticky Ribs

- 2 racks baby back ribs
- 1 cup dark brown sugar
- 2 tablespoons salt
- 1 tablespoon pepper
- 1 tablespoon garlic powder
- 1 tablespoon onion powder
- 1 tablespoon cayenne pepper
- 1 tablespoon paprika
- 2 tablespoons butter
- 1 tablespoon minced garlic
- 1 cup ketchup
- 1 cup apple cider vinegar
- 1 cup beef broth
- ¼ cup hot sauce
- ¼ cup Worcestershire sauce
- 3 tablespoons honey

Using a sharp knife, remove silver skin from ribs along the rack. Rinse ribs and thoroughly pat dry. In a small bowl, combine the dark brown sugar, salt, pepper, garlic powder, onion powder, cayenne pepper and paprika. Sprinkle the spice mixture all over the ribs, being liberal

with coverage. Allow to set for 10-15 minutes at room temperature while the sauce is being prepared. In a medium saucepan over low heat, add remaining ingredients and simmer for 20 minutes, stirring every 2-3 minutes. Remove from heat and cover with a lid. Heat one side of grill to medium-high heat. Place ribs on opposite side so that the ribs cook over indirect heat. Baste ribs every 10 minutes with BBQ Sauce for a total cooking time of 45-55 minutes. Remove ribs from heat and double wrap in aluminum foil. Return to grill on low heat and cook for an additional 20-25 minutes. Remove from grill and allow to rest for 10 minutes before slicing.

Strawberries are the angels of the earth—innocent and sweet with green leafy wings reaching heavenward. ~Terri Guillemets

SHADE and RUNA

Hell Frozen Over Smoothie Pops

Meatloaf and Monster Mash Cupcakes

Chicken Parmesan

Cauliflower Pizza

Seafood Platter
Fried Shrimp, Fried Catfish, Buttermilk Hush Hellhound Puppies and Beer Battered Fries

Slice of Life

SHADE AND RUNA

The rich, sweet aroma of vanilla made Runa's mouth water as she turned on the professional quality electric mixer her mate, Shade, had gotten her for Christmas. She wasn't a big fan of cooking meals, but she did enjoy baking sweet treats, and her family didn't complain a bit.

Boots clomped on the floor down the hall, and she turned off the mixer as Shade sauntered into the kitchen. He'd donned his black paramedic uniform for his afternoon shift at Underworld General Hospital, and she had a powerful urge to rip it off. Right here in the kitchen. She could finish making cookies to go with the smoothie pops she'd just put in the freezer to celebrate Stryke's A+ in science class later.

"Where are the boys?" he asked as he reached for a bottle of water in the fridge.

"They're at Stewie's pool party. Serena just sent a picture of them playing on the big float. It's on my phone if you want to see it."

"We should get a pool," he said as he swiped his finger across her phone's screen.

"We're welcome to use theirs anytime," she pointed out.

A smile ruffled his lips at the sight of the three dark-haired, espresso-eyed boys, the spitting images of their father, splashing in the water.

"Wraith and Serena made their house *the* place to be when they put it in, didn't they?"

It was probably the very reason they put in the pool. "Well, they love parties and kids."

"That's because they only have one," he muttered, but he was joking. Shade adored children, and when they were around, he could always be found nearby.

She fetched a can of cooking spray from a cupboard. "Speaking of kids, this morning a witch at the hospital told me I'm going to have twins in exactly eight years."

"Only twins?" Shade twisted the cap off his water. "Awesome."

She shook a spatula at him. "I remember when you wanted a whole bunch of kids."

"I remember too," Shade said. "And then we had triplets."

"Are you saying you don't want more?"

Pausing with the bottle at his lips, he shrugged. "We've got centuries ahead of us. I'm not in a hurry."

Neither was she. She loved being a mother, but she only had so much time between volunteering at the hospital and taking care of triplets, a mate, and two homes. Granted, one of the homes was a cave in a jungle, but it still had modern appliances and conveniences like hot running water and toilets, and modern things needed to be cleaned.

"I still can't believe your drive to impregnate me hasn't kicked in since the boys were born."

"That's how it works when we're mated." He grabbed a granola bar from the pantry and tucked it into the leg pocket of his BDU pants. "The drive only kicks in when our mates are ready. You're clearly not ready."

"You think? I barely have time to shower, let alone have more kids. But I'm sure everything will be different in eight years," she added, with more than a little sarcasm.

"You never know." He waggled his brows. "Wanna practice making our twins?"

Always up for a little practice, Runa eyed her mate, her body already heating at the thought of watching him strip out of his uniform. Or maybe she'd make him leave it on. It was sexy as hell.

"Don't you have to be at work in fifteen minutes?" she asked.

"Con will cover for me. Sin's working late with DART today."

Smiling, she peeled off her shirt and tossed it at him. "Then by all means...let's get some practice in."

Shade lay in the afterglow of their lovemaking, knowing he needed to get to work. But even after nearly a decade with Runa, every day still felt like they were on their honeymoon, and he didn't want to leave her.

Of all his siblings, he was the one who had fallen the most headfirst into family life.

He loved it. He loved everything about it. He was the PTA-attending soccer dad, and if Eidolon hadn't needed him so much during the triplets' early years, he would have been a happy stay-at-home dad. As it was, almost all of his days off were spent doing family things, from day trips to museums and theme parks to teaching the boys how to fish, how to perform first aid and, given that they were demons who would have to defend themselves from other underworlders, how to fight.

And yesterday on his day off, he taught them how to make meatloaf cupcakes for dinner. Blade was a picky eater who wasn't a fan of meatloaf, but Shade had discovered that he'd eat any food that could be made into a cupcake.

"We're the best parents, aren't we?"

Runa turned toward him as she lay in the crook of his arm, her head resting on his biceps, covering three generational glyphs on his dermoire. "Hmm?"

"Of all my brothers' families. Like, we're the most normal."

She gave him a placating smile. "Depends how you define normal. Our bedroom at the cave is a BDSM chamber, and once a month I turn into a werewolf."

She had a point, but that wasn't *the* point. "You know what I mean." Taking her hand, he twined his fingers with hers. They were so delicate, but so incredibly strong. "I think we're pretty awesome."

"We are." She wiggled closer. "But I might be biased."

He stroked the soft skin on the back of her hand and stared up at the ceiling fan as it spun in lazy circles. "It's weird how we all turned out so different. My brothers, and I, I mean. As parents."

"I don't know." Runa thought about it for a second. "You and Lore are a lot alike. You're both doting and patient."

Lore had the patience of a saint. Mace was a handful, a mini-Wraith with an overabundance of attitude and mischief.

"Actually, you're all pretty patient with the kids," she continued.

"Yeah, but there are different kinds of patient. Wraith's is like, meh, Stewie will do it when he's ready. And Eidolon?" Shade snorted. "He's not as patient as he is stubborn. He'll wait as long as it takes for you to do what he wants, but you pay for every floofing minute you delay."

Runa laughed. "Tayla says he's relentlessly stubborn."

"Poor Sabre." Tayla was less strict than Eidolon, but they were both pretty intense, Type-A and focused.

"Oh, I think Sabre is fine," Runa said as she began to trace circles on his abs, just above where the sheet lay across his hips. "With his temperament, he thrives in that kind of environment. Could you imagine a kid like Stryke having Eidolon as a father?"

Oh, hell, no. "E would destroy Stryke."

Stryke was the most sensitive and easygoing of their sons, a true mama's boy with a good heart. Rade was the spirited one, the troublemaker and ringleader for most of the hot water they got into. Blade was a mix of his brothers and of the three of them, the one most like Shade.

Runa pushed herself up on one elbow. "You know, I was talking to Serena the other day, and she brought up a good point. All our children will be brought up in stable, loving families, largely in human society. It'll be so different than what you and your brothers, or even most Seminus demons, grew up with."

"I was raised in a stable, loving family of Umber demons," he protested. "Until they were slaughtered and eaten by another demon." He glanced over at her. "Yeah, yeah, I made your point." Her kiss-swollen lips curved in a self-satisfied smile. "So you think our kids are going to be so well adjusted that they grow up and have boring, uneventful lives?"

"Boring and uneventful? In our family?" She chuckled. "Never. But they won't have the kind of obstacles to happiness that you all had."

Obstacles to happiness. Otherwise known as trauma.

But no, none of the children in his family would know trauma if he could help it. Life was full of surprises, but he and Runa, and all his siblings, had laid solid foundations for their families. They had, in fact, played a part in saving the world so the kids had a chance at all.

So Shade, figuring he had nothing to worry about, at least for right now, agreed with his mate, the female of his dreams, and turned off his cell phone.

Runa gave him a goofy smile. "What are you doing?"

He rolled over and, before she could blink, tucked her beneath him. "I'm playing hooky."

"Nice." Her smile turned naughty and her arms came up to wrap around his neck. "For how long?"

"For as long as you want. Con owes me several shifts." He brushed his mouth over hers. "And then when you're done with me...let's talk about getting a pool..."

For Runa and Shade's romantic beginning (it actually wasn't a romantic beginning at all...full of dungeons and monsters and betrayal, you know, the usual things), check out book 2 of the Demonica series, Desire Unchained!

Family Friendly Food

Hell Frozen Over Smoothie Pops

2 cups frozen blueberries

2 tablespoons honey

¼ cup milk

2 cups vanilla Greek yogurt

In a food processor, add frozen blueberries, honey and milk and pulse until smooth. Pour into a large bowl and fold in Greek yogurt. Fill 8-10 popsicle molds and insert popsicle sticks. Freeze for 4 hours before serving.

To make a more layered popsicle, do not fold in Greek yogurt with the blueberries. Simply layer the two in the popsicle molds.

Meatloaf and Monster Mash Cupcakes

2 pounds ground beef

2 eggs

¼ cup Worcestershire sauce

1 cup ketchup

1 tablespoon mayonnaise

¼ cup chopped sweet onion

1 box cornbread stuffing mix

1 cup shredded cheddar cheese

Topping

6 cups Mashed Potatoes

Chopped parsley

Preheat oven to 350 degrees. Mix together all ingredients and distribute evenly in a 12-cup muffin tin. Bake for 25 minutes.

Top with Mashed Potatoes. To resemble a "cupcake," add the mashed potatoes to a piping bag with a star tip. Pipe onto each meatloaf cupcake and sprinkle with parsley.

Mashed Potatoes

6 russet potatoes, cut into 1-inch cubes

8 tablespoons (1 stick) butter

1 (12 ounce) can evaporated milk

¼ cup mayonnaise

1 tablespoon garlic powder

Salt and pepper to taste

In a large stock pot, bring a pot of water to a boil. Add potatoes and boil until they are fork tender, usually about 20 minutes. Drain the water and add remaining ingredients. Mash with a potato masher and serve. For a creamier potato, you can use an electric hand mixer. Add remaining can of evaporated milk if not creamy enough, depending on size of potatoes.

Chicken Parmesan

- 2 cups oil
- 2 cups plus 1 cup flour
- 4 cups milk
- 1 tablespoon garlic powder
- 1 tablespoon onion powder
- 1 tablespoon salt
- 1 teaspoon pepper
- 4-6 thin boneless skinless chicken breasts
- 1 (16 ounce) box angel hair pasta
- 2 fresh mozzarella balls, sliced
- 1 batch Marinara
- 1 batch Parmesan Sauce

In a large skillet over medium high heat, bring oil to 350 degrees. Place 1 cup of flour in a large bowl, milk in a separate large bowl and remaining 2 cups of flour in a large bowl. Add garlic powder, onion powder, salt and pepper to the 2 cups of flour and stir to combine. Dredge each piece of chicken in the plain flour then milk then seasoned flour. Place 3-4 pieces of chicken in the skillet at a time and fry on each side for 3-4 minutes or until the internal temperature is 165 degrees. Drain on paper towels. While the chicken is frying, bring a large pot of water to a boil. Add the pasta and boil for 6-8 minutes or until pasta is cooked through. Place the chicken on a cookie sheet and top with 2 slices each of mozzarella. Place in the oven and broil for 2-3 minutes or until cheese has melted. To serve, place about 1 cup of pasta on a plate and top with marinara. Add one piece of chicken and top with additional marinara and 2-3 tablespoons of Parmesan Sauce.

Parmesan Sauce

- 1 tablespoon butter
- 2 tablespoons flour
- 3 cups chicken broth
- ½ teaspoon salt
- ¼ teaspoon pepper
- 1 cup freshly grated Parmesan

In a small saucepan over low heat, melt butter then whisk in flour. Stir until combined then slowly add in chicken broth. Whisk until thickened, about 1-2 minutes. Add salt, pepper and Parmesan. Stir until combined then remove from heat.

Marinara

- 12 ripe Roma tomatoes
- 1 (28 ounce) can whole peeled San Marzano tomatoes
- ¼ cup olive oil
- 1 onion, diced
- 2 celery ribs, diced
- 2 tablespoons minced garlic
- 1 tablespoon tomato paste
- 1 teaspoon salt
- 2 teaspoons sugar
- 1 teaspoon dried basil
- 1 teaspoon dried oregano
- 1 tablespoon dried parsley
- 1 teaspoon white wine vinegar

In a large pot with 4-6 cups of water, add in Roma tomatoes. Bring to a boil for 1 minute then remove from heat. Pour off hot water and replace with cold water. Allow to cool. Remove the tops of the tomatoes with a knife and peel off all remaining skin. Add to a food processor with the can of undrained San Marzano tomatoes. Pulse on low until completely pureed. In a Dutch oven over low heat, add the olive oil, onion, celery and garlic. Simmer for 10-15 minutes or until translucent and tender. Stir in tomato paste until blended. Add in tomatoes and remaining ingredients. Simmer for 2 hours, stirring frequently.

QUICK TIP

If you are unable to find "thin" chicken breasts simply cut a chicken breast in half.

Cauliflower Pizza

- 1 head cauliflower
- 1 egg
- 1 teaspoon dried oregano
- 1 teaspoon dried basil
- ¼ teaspoon salt
- ¼ teaspoon pepper
- ½ cup grated Parmesan
- 1 cup fresh spinach
- 4-6 cherry tomatoes, sliced
- 1 cup freshly grated Parmesan

Preheat oven to 375 degrees. Separate cauliflower into florets. Chop florets into smaller pieces and add to a food processor. Pulse until cauliflower is completely pureed and resembles a rice mixture. Spread cauliflower on a parchment lined cookie sheet. Bake for 15 minutes. Remove from oven and place in a cheesecloth. Squeeze the liquid out of the cauliflower into a bowl. Squeeze until you can't squeeze anymore. It needs to have as much liquid out as possible. Increase the oven temperature to 450 degrees. In a large bowl, add the egg and seasonings. Whisk together with a fork, then add the ½ cup of Parmesan and cauliflower. When combined, place on a parchment-lined round pizza pan. Flatten with your hands until you've formed a thin crust. Bake for 20 minutes. Flip the crust over and top with fresh spinach, sliced tomatoes and Parmesan. Return to oven and bake until cheese is melted.

Seafood Platter

A seafood platter can be mixed with a number of varieties. Here are a few of my favorites.

Fried Shrimp

- 6 cups oil for frying
- 4 eggs
- 1 cup milk
- 1 cup flour
- 1 cup cornmeal
- 1 teaspoon salt
- 1 teaspoon pepper
- 2 pounds shrimp, peeled and deveined

In a Dutch oven or deep fryer, bring oil to 350 degrees. In a large bowl, whisk together the eggs and milk. Next, mix together the flour, cornmeal, salt and pepper. Dredge about 10 shrimp at a time in the egg mixture and then cover in the dry flour mixture. Shake off the excess and place in oil. Fry for 1 to 2 minutes or until shrimp are pink. Continue with remaining shrimp and place on paper towels to drain. Serve with cocktail sauce.

Fried Catfish

1 cup sour cream

2 cups whole milk

2 cups flour

1 cup cornmeal

¼ cup Cajun seasoning

10-12 catfish fillets

Oil for frying

Combine sour cream and milk in a mixing bowl. In a separate bowl, mix together the flour, cornmeal and Cajun seasoning. In a Dutch oven or deep fryer, bring oil to 350 degrees. Dredge each piece of fish in the wet mixture and then in the dry mixture. Place 1-2 pieces of fish in the oil and fry for about 4-6 minutes until done. Repeat with remaining fish. Drain on paper towels.

Buttermilk Hush Hellhound Puppies

1 (2 pound) bag Hush Puppy mix

1 onion, diced

1 bottled beer

½ cup buttermilk

6 cups oil, for frying

In a large bowl, combine all ingredients except for oil. Let sit for 15-20 minutes. Heat oil to 350 degrees in a deep fryer or Dutch oven. Drop 1 tablespoon of batter into oil and fry until golden brown, about 1-2 minutes. Fry 4-6 at a time until all batter is used. Drain on paper towels.

Beer Battered Fries

6 cups oil for frying

1 cup flour

½ cup cornstarch

1 teaspoon garlic powder

1 teaspoon onion powder

1 teaspoon paprika

1 teaspoon salt

1 teaspoon pepper

1 bottled beer (AmberBock is great)

6 russet potatoes, peeled and cut into ½-inch thick strips

Fill a Dutch oven or deep fryer with oil and heat over medium heat until oil reaches 350 degrees. Line a baking sheet with paper towels. In a medium bowl, whisk together the flour, cornstarch, garlic powder, onion powder, paprika, salt and pepper. Add 1 cup of beer and stir until smooth, adding more beer if needed. Batter should coat the back of a spoon. Set aside. Place the potatoes in the oil, in 3-4 batches. Cook until golden brown, about 5 minutes. Use a slotted spoon to remove and drain on paper towels. Place the partially cooked fries a few at a time in the batter to coat. Then place in the oil and use tongs to keep them separate and not stuck together. Cook until deep golden brown, 2 to 3 minutes. Remove and place on paper towels to drain. Sprinkle with additional salt.

RESEPH *and* JILLIAN

Chicken Biscuit Pot Pie

Cherry Hand Pies

Taco Spaghetti

Fried Mac and Cheese Bites

French Onion Soup

Soft Shell Crab BLT

If junk food is the devil, then a sweet orange is as scripture.
~Terri Guillemets

RESEPH AND JILLIAN

Jillian loved all the seasons in Colorado, but fall was her favorite. At least, it was her favorite until winter, which was her favorite until spring. Which was her favorite until summer. Which was her favorite until fall.

She just really loved Colorado.

Which was why the decision she'd just made was so painful.

"What do you think Reseph is going to say about this?"

Jillian put down the pitchfork she'd been using to spread straw around the barn and glanced over at her best friend, Stacey. "I think he'll be thrilled."

Stacey leveled a *get serious* look at Jillian. "The guy is a nudist who likes his privacy. Two things that don't go together, but, well...it's Reseph. Do you honestly think he's going to want to move to a big city?"

"Yes," Jillian said, a little defensively. One of the goats let out what she swore was a dubious bleat.

"Okay." Stacey shrugged. "You know him better than I do."

Every one of Stacey's words dripped with doubt, irritating Jillian more than it should have. Maybe because she herself was experiencing a niggle of doubt.

Before Jillian met Reseph, the fourth Horseman of the Apocalypse, his need for isolation and privacy had been so encompassing that he'd lived in a mountain cave. And yet, he wasn't shy or antisocial. If anything, he loved activity and parties...but in his downtime, he wanted to be completely shut off from the outside world, which was why her remote little hobby farm in the Rockies was so appealing to him.

"Come on." Jillian shoved open the barn door and stepped into the sunny but cool and windy fall day. "I made a big pot of French onion soup and some homemade bread for lunch."

Stacey perked up. "Yum. I'm starving. And I think it's sweet how you cook meals even when Reseph's gone, just in case he comes home."

With a sigh that didn't come close to conveying how much she missed Reseph, Jillian slid the barn door closed. He'd been gone for a couple of weeks, drawn by a plague in China that had killed hundreds.

"The plague seems to be winding down. He could be home any day now." She hoped so, anyway. Reseph wouldn't want to miss the first snow of the season or Cara and Ares's baby shower on Saturday.

A chilly wind tore through the trees as if to warn her that the first snow was coming soon. Stacey stuffed her hands in her coat pockets as they started down the path toward the house.

"One of the downfalls of being married to the Horseman known as Pestilence, I guess," Stacey said.

Jillian shuddered at the mention of Reseph's evil name. She'd been on the receiving end of Pestilence's cruelty when Reseph's Seal had broken, unleashing his inner demon and nearly starting the Apocalypse. If not for his siblings, Thanatos, Ares, and Limos, and their efforts to keep their own Seals from breaking, the world would be a very different place right now.

"I guess," Jillian agreed.

"It's still seems so bizarre that my best friend is married to one of the Four Horsemen of the Apocalypse." Stacey shook her head in awe. "And you have a werewolf servant."

Once again, Jillian shuddered. He was a slave, not a servant. A servant had a choice. Tracker didn't. He'd been sold into slavery as an infant, and she'd been bonded to him without her knowledge or consent. That it had been an act of kindness that had ultimately benefitted them both didn't make the reality of the situation any less shitty.

"Speaking of Tracker..." Lowering her voice, Stacey glanced around the yard. "Where is he?"

Jillian cast her friend a curious look. Stacey had never asked about Tracker before. "Why?"

"Just wondering."

"Because..."

Stacey's pale cheeks were already pink from the cold, but now they turned ripe-apple red. "No reason."

So full of shit. "Uh-huh."

Stacey snorted. "What? Don't look at me like that. He's spoken like three words to me in the last two years." She cast a wistful gaze at the cabin. "But damn, he looks good without a shirt."

On that, Stacey was not wrong. Tracker usually worked around the house in nothing but boots and jeans, his big, sinewy body on full display. Of course, she could say the same about Reseph, except he was usually as naked from the waist down as he was from the waist up.

Jillian didn't complain. At all. Although it was a little embarrassing when UPS dropped off packages.

"Oh, damn." Stacey stopped on the path, patting her pockets as if missing something. "I left my sunglasses in the barn. I'll grab them and meet you in the house."

Jillian hadn't taken more than a dozen steps when light flashed inside the circular stone landing site ahead. Any one of the Horsemen could use it, but she held her breath, hoping it would be Reseph who would emerge from the gate.

A curtain of shimmering light parted and Reseph stepped out, his long platinum hair spilling over armor that gleamed in the sun, his cool blue eyes focused like lasers on Jillian.

She didn't even have a chance to speak before he was on her, taking her to the ground in a smooth tackle that would have hurt had he not twisted at the last second to take the brunt of the impact.

"I missed you," he growled against her mouth.

Arching into him, her heart thumping with joy, she wrapped her arms around his neck. "I've missed you too."

"I didn't," Stacey called out in a teasing voice as she headed toward her truck. "Jillian, we'll do lunch another time. See you later!"

Reseph didn't even look up from nuzzling her neck. "Bedroom," he rasped. "Now."

Jillian couldn't think of anything she'd love more.

Reseph lay on the bed, his legs tangled in the sheets, his fingers tangled with Jillian's. The sex had been crazy intense, and he wouldn't be surprised to see gouges in the hardwood floor from the scooting of the bed across it.

"You okay?" he rasped, exhaustion and post-coital bliss making his voice rough.

"Mm-hmm." Jillian's eyes were closed, her kiss-ravaged mouth tipped up in a smile, her dark hair spilled across the blue flannel pillow case.

Must be November. Jillian always switched the sheets from satin to flannel on Halloween night. He used to think it was weird, but he'd learned to appreciate the cozy warmth when he climbed into bed with her on chilly nights.

He pressed a kiss against her forehead and inhaled the delicate scent of the pumpkin spice shampoo she brought out of storage every year with the sheets. "Sorry about the insanity."

"I know," she murmured. "It's all right. I understand how you're affected by certain events."

She was so perfect. She accepted him flaws and all. And being the product of the union between a sex demon and an angel bred for battle was definitely a flaw. Well, that and the minor thing about terrorizing and nearly killing her a while back.

Bringing her hand to his, he kissed her knuckles. Before this day was over, he was going to kiss every inch of her. Maybe more than once.

"I'm going to shower. And then I'm going to eat whatever smells so good in the kitchen." He pressed another lingering kiss into the soft skin of her hand. "And then I'm going to eat *you*."

He hopped out of bed and got into the shower, eager to wash away the events of the last two weeks. The plague had been of natural origin, not caused by demons or man or, thankfully, himself as Pestilence, which somehow made a difference in how crazy it made him and how long it took him to recover. After a few meals, a few rounds of sex, and a few hours of sleep, he'd be back to normal and would be rid of the death-hangover that was, even now, pounding like a four-armed troll against the inside his skull.

Moaning at the luxury of being clean, Reseph stood under the spray until the hot water ran out. He needed to remember to get a bigger hot water tank before winter set in, one that would complement the steam shower he was going to talk Jillian into. The cabin was already his favorite place in the world, but with a few tweaks, it would be absolute paradise.

Stomach growling, he swiped a towel over himself in a half-assed dry job and threw on a pair of shorts. Jillian insisted on pants, pajamas, or a robe at the table. Humans were funny that way.

He found her in the kitchen, her lush body wrapped in the fuzzy cream robe he'd bought her for Christmas as part of a spa package. She'd set out two steaming bowls of soup, a loaf of homemade bread, and a bottle of beer for him, a sparkling water for her.

"I've missed your cooking," he said as he plopped down in his usual spot.

"If I'd known you'd be home today I'd have made something more substantial. I know you don't eat when you're called away like that."

His stomach growled again, right on cue. He hadn't eaten in two weeks, and now that he could smell food instead of sickness and death, his body was waking up with a vengeance.

He didn't even bother with a spoon. The first bowl of soup went down like a mug of ale. After following that with half the loaf of bread, he managed to eat the second and third bowls of soup with a spoon. By the time he'd ladled up his fourth serving, his stomach had quit growling and he didn't feel as much like a winter-starved bear coming out of hibernation.

"Did anything interesting happen while I was gone?"

"Nope." Jillian shook her head. "And before you ask, yes, your brothers and Limos came to check on me every day, even though I have Tracker just next door."

Reseph was more grateful for Tracker than he could even say. The werewolf was completely dedicated to Jillian, and not because of the slave bond. He truly loved her, probably because she was the only master he'd ever had who treated him not as a slave, but as family. She didn't require anything from him and in fact, she was constantly trying to get him to relax and do things for himself, but the only time he took for his own needs was during the three nights of the werewolf moon.

"There was a full moon while I was gone," Reseph pointed out. "He couldn't protect you while he's out running with his pack or chained in his basement."

"Reseph," she sighed as she reached for her mug of hot cocoa, "it was fine. Stacey was here a lot too."

Stacey? That was a floofing laugh. "Stacey would faint at the sight of a tiny little spiny hellrat. How the hell can she help if you're attacked by demons?"

Jillian huffed in mock annoyance. Probably mock annoyance. Reseph and Stacey had gotten off to an awkward start, and they'd never gotten past it. Reseph had never even tried. He liked their friendly rivalry and was glad Jillian had a close friend who knew the truth about the underworld. At Reaver's request, Stacey was one of the few humans whose memories hadn't been altered by angels to explain the Apocalyptic events in ways that didn't involve demons. Most humans now believed the millions who died when his Seal broke, setting off the beginnings of the Apocalypse, had actually succumbed to disease and localized war.

Apparently, there were plans to start revealing the truth to humans over a gradual period of time, but Reseph really didn't care. He liked his life out here in the middle of nowhere, where he didn't get bombarded with news and human drama all the time.

Life was so good. He wouldn't change a single thing.

"I'm not going to get attacked by demons," Jillian said, with a roll of her bright green eyes. "We have so many layers of protection here. If the wards don't stop them, I've got Tracker as well as a direct line to three other Horsemen and an angel or two." She put down her spoon and inhaled before saying softly, "But if you're worried about me being out here when you're gone, I have a solution."

His heart gave an excited kick against his ribs. "Are you finally going to go stay with my sister or one of my brothers?" He'd been trying to get her to do that for years.

"No." She took another deep breath, and this time when his heart kicked, it was with sudden dread. "Don't freak out, okay?"

Man, that was a surefire way to make him freak out, but somehow he managed to keep himself level. "What is it?"

Jillian, his beautiful, perfect mate, smiled…and ruined his day.

"I want to move."

Jillian held her breath as she waited for Reseph's reaction. At first, he seemed to take it well. He simply watched as her cat, Doodle, jumped into her lap and stuck his little brown head into her bowl.

Then, as Doodle flicked his paw in dismissal at the soup, Reseph gripped the edge of the table as if trying to steady it. Or as if trying to steady himself.

"You want to do what?"

Maybe she should have waited to dump this on him until after he'd recovered from the plague, but she'd never been good at keeping things from him and besides, she was excited about this. She just had to get him on board.

"I know this is sudden, but I've been thinking about it for months." She stroked Doodle's soft fur, eliciting a contented purr from him. "I want to move to a city. Berlin or Paris or Amsterdam. Maybe Sydney. Or Stockholm."

Reseph's handsome face was uncharacteristically expressionless. Usually every emotion he felt played out in his clear blue eyes and in the set of his made-for-sin mouth. Which meant he was intentionally controlling his feelings, and that was never good.

"No."

She blinked. "No? We can't even discuss it?"

"There's nothing to discuss." Shoving to his feet, he grabbed his bowl. "Cities are stupid and full of people."

"Oh, well, there's a legit argument," she muttered. "Cities are stupid."

He took his bowl over to the sink and turned on the water. "I just don't know why you'd want to make such a drastic move. What brought this on?"

Jillian twisted around in her seat so she could talk to him, but his back was to her as he rinsed his bowl with brisk, jerky movements. "A lot of things, really. Part of it is that I'm tired of being a hermit."

"We can travel more." He swung around to her, his abs and arms glistening from water spray. On his forearm, the tattoo-like glyph of his war stallion, Conquest, stomped its feet in agitation, sensing his master's mood. "If you wanted to spend more time in a city, you should have told me. Let's get dressed and go. Anywhere you want. We can be there in thirty seconds."

"It's not the same, Reseph." She placed Doodle on the floor and stood. "I love traveling with you, but I just...I want a change. We can sell this place and--"

"Sell it?" Reseph croaked. "You want to get rid of your family home? The house you grew up in?"

There were things she'd miss about the house, but it had been her parents' dream home, not hers. "I have plenty of memories and pictures. It's no big deal."

"No big deal?" He made an angry, sweeping gesture with his arm. "You've got thirty years of history here. You don't just throw that away."

"I'm not throwing anything away." She moved toward him, but he scooted past her to grab another beer from the fridge. "Everything that's important will move with us."

"What about the animals? What about Sammy? Conquest loves him."

"I've already made arrangements with Stacey. We'll take Doodle, and she'll take the rest of the animals. We can visit anytime we want."

He shook his head. "No."

"Reseph--"

"No!" He slammed his beer down on the counter without opening it. "We're not moving, and that's final."

"Nothing is final," she snapped. "And I don't appreciate your attitude."

"Selling things is final," he shot back. "And you don't just throw away things because they're no longer convenient."

"No longer convenient? What are you talking about? This is about making a positive change. I'm immortal now. I can take some risks. Do things I might have been afraid to do before." She made a pleading gesture with her hands. "Let's do this, Reseph. Let's take a new adventure together."

"Or you'll take one by yourself?"

Taken aback, she stared, unable to fathom his words. "By myself? No, of course not. Where is this coming from?"

Cursing, Reseph shook his head. "I need a minute. Just...give me a minute."

With that, he stormed out of the kitchen and then out of the house.

Reseph couldn't believe how rattled he was by Jillian's bombshell announcement. How could she want to move? How could she want to abandon her old life?

And making it worse, Limos was siding with Jillian.

"Reseph, I know you're upset, but is it really that big of a deal?" From the deck of her Hawaiian beach house, Limos kept a watchful eye on her mate, Arik, as he strolled along the sand with their daughter. Keilani, her mother's daughter in every way, was keeping Arik busy as she ran from place to place gathering seashells.

"Jillian grew up there," he said. "It was her parents' place. It was where she went to stay safe after..." After Pestilence and his minions attacked her. "How can she just give it up like it was nothing?"

Limos turned to him, the salty ocean breeze whipping her black hair around her face. "I don't think this is about Jillian at all," she said as she tied her hair back with the lime and yellow scrunchie thing she'd worn around her wrist.

"Then what the hell would it be about?"

"Duh," Limos huffed. "It's about you and your past."

"You think I'm still hung up on my childhood?"

"Reseph, you've always had abandonment issues--"

Oh, criminy, not that shit again. If he so much as mentioned that he hated milk, Limos would claim it was related to his birth mother leaving him before he'd been able to breastfeed or his adoptive mother leaving him before he was done breastfeeding.

He really did hate milk and both his mothers, though. Still didn't prove anything.

"You know what was great about the past?" He watched Keilani do a face plant in the sand and then bound back to her feet with a delighted squeal. His niece had a great sense of humor already. "No one used terms like 'abandonment issues' or 'narcissist.' Or 'psychopath.'" He shrugged. "Just saying."

"I'm serious." Limos pointed an accusatory finger at him. "Almost everything is disposable to you. But you glom hard onto things that represent stability. Don't look at me like that. You know I'm right." She waved at Keilani and then turned back to Reseph. "You found a home at Jillian's mountain retreat, so you're glomming. You're just glomming the wrong thing."

"Huh?"

"Argh." Limos cuffed him on the shoulder. "Home isn't a cabin or wooded property, dumbass. Home is wherever Jillian goes. Glom *her.*"

As much as he hated to admit it, his sister was right. But still, the thought of leaving the place where he'd lived his happiest years gave him heartburn.

Maybe they could compromise. He'd flipped out before they could even talk about it. Because he was a dumbass, like Limos said. They could still move to whatever city Jillian wanted to move to but keep the Colorado property for vacations. Or if he needed to escape people.

That might work. The very idea certainly helped ease the burn in his chest. "Thanks for talking me down, sis. You're like a living, breathing Alka-Seltzer."

"Aw, aren't you sweet in your own weird way."

"Yeah, well, now I have to show Jillian how sweet I am. I totally freaked out. I was such a jerk."

Limos cocked a black eyebrow. "Don't tell me it was your first fight?"

"Nah," he said. "I'm always doing stupid shit. But this was our worst fight. And it was all my fault." He glanced down the beach at Arik. "When he floofs up, what does he do to get off the couch?"

She grinned, and something told him she liked it when Arik had to make it up to her for something. No doubt she enjoyed making his life hell.

"He changes diapers and gets up with Keilani at night, but I guess since you don't have a kid, that won't work." She tapped her chin thoughtfully. "What's something she always does for you?" She held up her hand as Reseph opened his mouth. "And I'm not talking about anything sexual.'

He snapped his mouth closed and thought about it. "She does everything inside the house, and I do all the outside stuff."

"Then you need to do some inside stuff. Do the laundry for her. Clean the house. Cook dinner. And tell her you're sorry." Li wiggled her fingers, making her flashy rings sparkle in the sunlight. "And expensive jewelry never hurts."

Okay, he could do all of that. Easy. He knew where the vacuum cleaner was, and he was pretty sure he could find the laundry soap. Dinner...that might be a little challenging.

"Do you have any good recipes? Easy recipes?"

"I have people who cook for me," Limos said. "But you should check out a show called Angel in the Kitchen. Harvester said you can look up recipes that will work for whatever purpose you want. Supposedly, they're infused with angel magic or some crap."

Reseph was willing to try anything at this point. And if he had to enlist the help of an angel to win over his own angel, he was all for it.

He eyed Limos. "Do you think you can help me out with something? I'm going to need to get Jillian out of the house for a few hours."

As expected, she was game.

Operation Apology was underway.

Reseph decided he wasn't cut out for domestic chores. He was much better at wielding a sword than a vacuum cleaner. And no matter how many times he mopped, the hardwood floors remained streaky. Worse, Doodle watched him like he was an idiot, all judgey and shit from his perch on the window sill.

Reseph couldn't even manage to do laundry right. He'd had to rinse a load twice to get rid of excess soap, and another load was completely ruined thanks to a little too much bleach.

He'd basically created more work with his dumbassery.

Surprisingly, however, cooking turned out to be his most successful attempt at showing Jillian how much she meant to him. In fact, the kitchen smelled heavenly and not like anything was burning or poisonous.

Cool.

He popped dessert into the oven and checked his watch. Jillian should be home any second. Limos had promised to gate her to the cabin as soon as they were done buying the Thanksgiving decorations Limos had insisted she'd needed Jillian's help with to pick out,, and she'd texted moments ago to say they were getting ready to head back.

Any second now...

The front door creaked open and slammed closed. Jillian was still pissed.

His pulse picked up, slinging adrenaline through his veins as if he were entering battle instead of preparing to negotiate an end to it.

Jillian appeared in the doorway to the kitchen. She was wearing one of his favorite outfits: worn jeans and a gauzy black blouse that emphasized her perfect breasts and long, slender neck, both of which he'd lavished with kisses hundreds of times. She'd taken off her shoes, her feet now encased in fluffy black slippers with skull and crossbones beads he'd given her for her birthday.

"Are you...are you actually cooking?"

"I'm attempting it, anyway."

"Why?"

Reseph had spent his entire life being a charming playboy, a lovable scamp that females loved. If there was ever a time to turn on his charm, it was now.

He grinned and shot her a wink as he checked on the Chicken Biscuit Pot Pie. "Because you deserve it." At her smile, he claimed victory. "Besides, I figured that if you could do it, I could too."

The smile fell off her face. "You what? You mean, if it's so easy that I can do it, surely you must be able to?"

"No! Of course not." Oh, shit, he'd taken his victory lap too soon. "That came out wrong. I meant that because you do it, I should too. I want to do my part. I want to do more."

"Is that why you think I want to move?" She drifted toward him, smelling of cinnamon and coffee. Limos must have stalled her at a coffee shop, knowing they were Jillian's weakness. "Because you don't do enough around here?"

He'd never really thought about that. "Well...now I'm wondering..."

She laughed, but it sounded a little bitter. "You do plenty around here, Reseph. You're always outside making improvements on the barn or the house. You do more with the animals than I do, and you look for any reason to go grocery shopping."

It was true. He loved grocery shopping. For most of his life, grocery stores hadn't existed. Now he found them to be wondrous places filled with a zillion kinds of ice cream and every spice imaginable. Sometimes when he got the urge to wander, he'd visit grocery stores in other countries just to see what kind of neat stuff they sold.

You could tell a lot about a country's people by what they bought in grocery stores.

The kitchen timer went off. Jillian's slippered feet whispered on the floor as she followed him to the oven.

"What are you making?"

"What am I attempting to make?" He mentally crossed his fingers in hopes that everything turned out. "I'm doing a pie themed dinner I found on the Angel in the Kitchen website. Chicken Biscuit Pot Pie and Cherry Hand Pies."

"Smells amazing."

He pulled the pot pie out of the oven and left the cherry pies to continue baking. "I hope it tastes like it smells. And like it looks."

Jillian came up behind him and peered at the bubbling dish. "I'm so hungry. I tried to get Limos to go to dinner, but she said she was busy."

"She had orders to bring you here," he said, a little sheepishly... exaggerated a bit to keep up the charm offensive. Ares had always said it was his best battle tactic, and he needed to use every weapon in his arsenal to make it up to Jillian.

Jillian's eyes shot wide as it dawned on her that she had been tricked. "She knew you were cooking?"

"I went to see her earlier," he admitted. "I needed to talk to her about our fight."

"That's funny," she murmured. "Because I talked to her about it too."

Well, that couldn't be good. "What did she say?"

"That you're a jackass." She gave him a pointed look, but her mouth was quirked in a small smile. "On that, we agree."

There was widespread agreement for that opinion. "I'm sorry, Jilly." He reset the timer for the cherry pies. "I overreacted. I was caught off guard and I panicked. But that was no excuse for treating you the way I did."

"It was my fault too." She sank down in a chair at the table. "I shouldn't have dumped it on you like that. I made a decision and didn't consult you about it first." Looking down at her freshly painted blue nails -- Limos must have taken her for a manicure as well -- she shook her head. "I think maybe I resent how much you're gone, and how much responsibility it leaves me with. I know it's not fair. You can't help it when you have to go. But I always feel like I've kind of been stranded."

He'd never really thought about what it was like for her when he was gone. He'd always been concerned about her safety, but her state of mind? Hadn't even occurred to him.

He was a selfish jerk sometimes, wasn't he?

Determined to make it up to her, he poured her a glass of wine and sat down across from her. "So what do we do now?"

"I think I might have a compromise."

They often operated on the same wavelength, probably because their minds had been linked together in order to preserve his sanity and keep Pestilence at bay. The wavelength had its drawbacks, but really, it kept them in sync a lot, and he suspected that now was one of those times.

"Let me guess," he said. "We move but keep this property for vacations and getaways?"

She nodded. "I can't believe I didn't think of it sooner."

It was definitely better than selling the place, but he also had another idea. "What about the other way around? We'll buy a place in any city in the world. You name it. It'll be our vacation spot."

Reaching for his hand, she gave a tiny shake of the head. "I'm ready for a change, Reseph. A big one. Buying a vacation home isn't a change."

Change was bad. The very idea, even with a compromise, made his gut churn. There was a reason he'd lived in a cave for centuries. He hung on to what he knew.

"Why do you want a change? Are you bored?"

"Trust me," she said wryly, "no one can be bored around you." Her fingernails clicked on her wine glass as she idly tapped the stem. "It's not that. It's just...I spread my wings a long time ago when I moved away. Being back here makes me feel like a teenager, like I'm trapped. I know we can go anywhere we want in a matter of seconds, but when you're gone for weeks at a time, I'm stuck here."

"You can call my sister or brothers. They'll take you anywhere you want." Even as his words faded, he knew the argument was old and lame and clearly, if it was what Jillian wanted, she'd have been calling his siblings all the time.

"I hate that, Reseph. I have to rely on them to get me home when I'm done with whatever I'm doing. It inconveniences them, and it makes me feel like I'm on a leash. But if we're living in a city I can walk to the closest café for a pastry. Or I can take a jog in a park. Or I can drive or take public transportation to any number of places. It's lonely here. And now that I'm taking flying lessons, I'd like to live near an airport. I want to fly charter flights for DART. I want to do something to contribute to the fight for our planet, you know?"

He couldn't manufacture a single argument for any of that, so he conceded defeat. After all, Jillian had sacrificed a lot for him, and maybe it was time for him to do the same. He loved this cabin, but he loved her more.

So instead of throwing a Keilani-sized tantrum, he pulled up his big boy pants – pants he was wearing in the kitchen for Jillian's sake – and announced that dinner was ready.

Jillian was starving, but as Reseph dished up the pot pie, her stomach rebelled. She hated fighting with him, and although he'd apologized and they were in the midst of talking things out, there was still a lot of tension in the air, wafting around the kitchen along with the mouthwatering aromas of savory chicken and sweet cherries.

She dragged her fork through the veggie-laden pie. "Reseph, why did you get so upset when I said I wanted to move?"

Silence stretched as he considered his answer. "Limos thinks it's because I have abandonment issues. She's probably right. But I think it's more than that." He glanced down at his bowl, a soft pink blush rising up in his cheeks. He wasn't one to talk about his feelings -- at least not openly. He joked a lot, but he didn't ever lay his emotions completely bare. "I think I was afraid that you wanting something new meant you wanted everything new."

"What, like a new husband?" At his barely discernible nod, her heart broke. He was so new to unconditional love that even after their years together he still expected to lose everything. "Listen to me, Reseph. Do you trust me?"

He looked up in surprise. "More than anyone in my life."

"Then trust me when I say that the only way you'll lose me is if you turn into Pestilence again." She paused and narrowed her eyes at him. "Or if you cheat on me."

She wasn't sure which would be worse. Pestilence was terrifying, his bloodlust and penchant for cruelty beyond comprehension. But the thought of Reseph with another female – human or otherwise – hurt her in places Pestilence could never reach.

"That will never happen," he growled, and the sudden, possessive intensity in his expression was as much a promise as his words. She recognized the smoky, predatory gleam in his eyes and knew he was no longer interested in food. He wanted to take his promises to the bedroom and claim her in the most primitive way he knew how.

Her skin heated at the thought, and she was tempted to take his hand and drag him there right now.

But they had to clear the air first.

She loaded her fork with pot pie. This conversation was going to end in the bedroom no matter what, so she'd better eat now or it could be hours before she managed to get back into the kitchen. "Do you want me to trust you when you say that?"

His voice still rumbled with erotic intent. "Of course."

"Then return the favor and never doubt my love for you. Also, thank you for wearing clothes while you were cooking. "She paused with the fork at her lips. "You did wear clothes, right?"

"I might be immortal," he said with an amused snort, "but there are parts of my body that don't respond well to heat."

Smiling, she took a bite and moaned in food bliss. "This is so good."

"Guaranteed by the Angel in the Kitchen chick to wrap you in comfort like a blanket made from the hide of a bone devil."

Jillian didn't know what a bone devil was, but she got the gist. "Well, it worked. Now I can't wait for dessert."

He waggled his blond brows. "I can't either."

It was no surprise that the individual cherry pies were merely the first dessert course. He served the second course in bed. And as they lay snuggled in the sheets recovering, Reseph served up another surprise: brochures from every city she'd mentioned.

Together they were going to forge a new path and share new dreams.

But they would always have Colorado.

Reseph and Jillian's book, Rogue Rider, was one of my favorite books to write. Reseph had been an evil villain for four books, starting with Sin Undone (book 5 of the Demonica series). He was absolutely unredeemable for the first three books of the Lords of Deliverance series, which meant that I had a challenge on my hands. If you want to see how I handled that challenge, check out the entire Lords of Deliverance series, starting with Eternal Rider!

COMFORT FOOD

Chicken Biscuit Pot Pie

1 rotisserie chicken

1 can cream of celery soup

½ cup chicken broth

1 (8.5 ounce) can diced potatoes

1 (8.5 ounce) can mixed peas and carrots

4 cups biscuit mix

1 cup Sprite

1 cup sour cream

8 tablespoons (1 stick) butter, melted

Preheat oven to 375 degrees. Shred chicken and place in a mixing bowl. Add cream of celery soup, chicken broth, diced potatoes, peas and carrots and mix well. Pour into a greased large iron skillet or a 9 x 13-inch baking dish. In a large bowl, mix together biscuit mix, Sprite, and sour cream. Drop biscuit dough by spoonfuls (2-3 tablespoons each) over the top of the chicken pot pie until all dough has been used and the entire pie is covered. Brush the biscuits with melted butter and bake for 20-25 minutes or until the biscuits are golden brown. Remove from oven and cool for 5 minutes before serving.

Cherry Hand Pies

3 cups frozen cherries, pitted

½ cup sugar

1 tablespoon cornstarch

1 lemon, juiced

2 sheets puff pastry, thawed

1 egg

¼ cup sugar

Preheat oven to 450 degrees. In a small saucepan over low heat add the cherries and sugar. Stir until sugar is dissolved, about 5 minutes. Add the cornstarch and lemon juice and continue to stir for about 3-5 minutes or until the sauce has thickened. Remove from heat and allow to cool completely. Unfold each sheet of puff pastry and cut along the 3 lines, then cut each sheet in half, giving you a total of 12 squares. Place 2-3 tablespoons of cherry filling in the center of each pastry square and fold one corner of dough over the filling to reach the other corner of pastry. Seal the seams with a fork and place on a parchment lined cookie sheet. Cut a small slit in the center of the pie. Repeat with remaining hand pies. In a small bowl, whisk together the egg with 2 tablespoons of water and brush over each pie. Sprinkle each pie with sugar. Bake for 12-15 minutes or until golden brown. Allow to cool before serving.

QUICK TIP

For future use, place the pies on the parchment lined baking sheet and freeze for 30 minutes. Remove from freezer and individually wrap in plastic wrap. Return to the freezer. When ready to bake, remove from freezer and place on a parchment lined baking sheet. Bake in a 450 degree oven for 15-18 minutes or until golden brown.

Taco Spaghetti

1 (16 ounce) box thin spaghetti

1 pound ground beef, cooked and drained

1 packet taco seasoning

1 can Ro-Tel

1 can cream of mushroom soup

1 (32 ounce) block of Velveeta cheese, cubed

2 cups shredded sharp cheddar

Topping

8 ounces sour cream

Candied Jalapeno Slices

Preheat oven to 350 degrees. Cook spaghetti according to package directions. In a large skillet over low heat, add ground beef, taco seasoning and ¼ cup water. Stir to combine and simmer for 2 minutes. Add in Ro-Tel, cream of mushroom soup, and Velveeta cheese. Stir until the cheese is melted and combined. Stir in spaghetti and place in a greased 9 x 13-inch casserole dish. Top with cheddar cheese and bake for 10 minutes. Top with sour cream and Candied Jalapeno Slices.

Candied Jalapeno Slices

5 cups sugar

2 cups apple cider vinegar

1 teaspoon turmeric

1 teaspoon celery seed

1 teaspoon minced garlic

30 jalapenos, sliced

In a large saucepan over medium heat, bring sugar and vinegar to a boil. When the sugar is dissolved, add the turmeric, celery seed and garlic, stirring constantly. Add in the jalapenos and continue to stir for 5 minutes. Remove jalapenos and place in 3 pint-sized mason jars. Continue to boil syrup for an additional 5 minutes. Remove from heat and fill each jar with remaining syrup. The jalapenos need to set for 2 weeks before being ready to serve. They will keep for 2 months refrigerated.

Fried Mac and Cheese Bites

1 tablespoon salt

1 (16 ounce) box elbow pasta

8 tablespoons (1 stick) butter

2 tablespoons flour

1 cup heavy cream

1 cup milk

2 cups plus 1 cup sharp cheddar cheese

1 (8 ounce) package cream cheese

1 teaspoon garlic, minced

1 teaspoon pepper

Preheat oven to 350 degrees. Bring 4 cups of salted (½ tablespoon) water to a boil. Add pasta and cook for 8-10 minutes or until the pasta is cooked through. Drain pasta and set aside. In a medium saucepan over low heat, melt the butter and gradually whisk in the flour until a roux forms. Add the heavy cream and milk, whisking constantly until thickened. Stir in 2 cups of cheddar cheese, cream cheese, garlic, the remaining ½ tablespoon of salt, and pepper. When the cheese sauce is smooth, stir in the cooked pasta. Pour into a 9 x 13-inch greased baking dish and top with remaining cheddar cheese. Bake for 15 minutes and serve.

To Make the Mac and Cheese Bites

Leftover Mac and Cheese

2 cups all-purpose flour

4 eggs

4 cups panko breadcrumbs

6 cups oil, for frying

Refrigerate leftover Mac and Cheese overnight. Cut into 1-inch squares and coat with flour. Place on a cookie sheet and refrigerate for 30 minutes. Heat oil to 350 degrees. In a medium bowl, whisk the eggs. In a separate medium bowl, add the panko breadcrumbs. Remove the squares from the refrigerator and dredge each one in the egg and then in the panko breadcrumbs. Place 4 squares at a time in the oil and fry 1-2 minutes or until golden brown. Drain on paper towels.

French Onion Soup

3 tablespoons olive oil

6 sweet onions, thinly sliced

2 tablespoons butter

1 teaspoon sugar

1 teaspoon salt

8 cups beef broth

1 tablespoon minced garlic

1 teaspoon dried thyme

½ cup dry white wine

1 teaspoon pepper

1 French baguette

6 thin slices of provolone cheese

In a Dutch oven, heat the olive oil on medium heat. Add the onions and toss to coat with the oil. Cook the onions, stirring often, until softened, about 15 to 20 minutes. Increase the heat to medium high. Add the butter and cook, stirring often, until the onions start to brown, about 15 more minutes. Then sprinkle with sugar (to help with the caramelization) and salt and continue to cook until the onions are well browned, about 10 to 15 more minutes. Add the beef broth, minced garlic, and thyme. Bring to a simmer, cover and cook for about 30 minutes. While the soup is simmering, line a baking sheet with parchment paper and preheat the oven to 450 degrees. Cut the baguette in 1-inch slices and brush both sides lightly with olive oil. Place in the oven and toast until lightly browned, about 5 to 7 minutes. To serve, ladle soup into oven safe bowls and place one slice of toasted baguette on top of each bowl of soup, followed by one slice of provolone. Place the bowls of soup under the broiler for 1-2 minutes or until the cheese is melted and bubbly. If you do not have oven safe bowls the steam from the soup will melt the cheese. Serve immediately.

Soft Shell Crab BLT

1 cup mayonnaise

1 lemon, juiced

½ teaspoon minced garlic

2 cups buttermilk

4 soft shell crabs, cleaned and rinsed

2 cups flour

1 tablespoon Cajun seasoning

2 cups oil, for frying

8 slices of bread, toasted

4 butter lettuce leaves

2 tomatoes, sliced

8 thick slices bacon, cooked

In a small bowl, combine the mayonnaise, lemon juice and garlic. Set aside until the building of the sandwich. In a large bowl, add the buttermilk and crabs. Refrigerate for 30 minutes. In a separate large bowl add the flour and Cajun seasoning. Dredge each crab in the flour mixture to coat. In a large iron skillet or heavy frying pan, heat oil to 350 degrees. Place 2 crabs at a time in the oil and fry for 3 minutes on each side. Drain on paper towels. To build the sandwich, spread the garlic mayonnaise on each slice of toasted bread, add one leaf of lettuce, 2 slices of tomato, 2 slices of bacon and top with soft shell crab. Top with 2nd slice of bread and serve. Repeat with remaining 3 sandwiches.

Vegetables are food of the earth, but fruits taste of the heavens.
~Terri Guillemets

ARES and CARA

Goat Cheese Truffles

Seven Layer Greek Goddess

Bacon Wrapped Stuffed Figs

Mini Chicken Gyros with Easy Tzatziki

Pot Stickers

Blueberry Lemon Angel Food Cake Trifle

Caramel Pretzel Bites

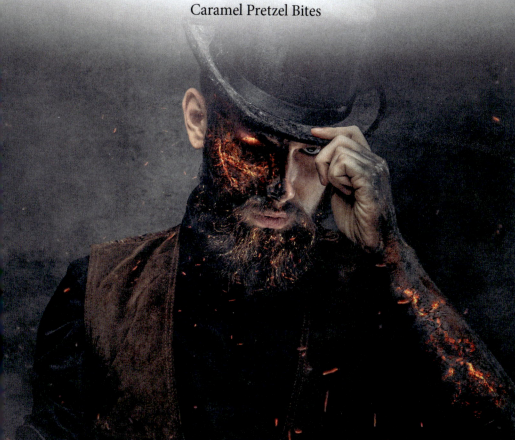

ARES AND CARA

Ares was in a panic. And as one of the Four Horsemen of the Apocalypse with eons of war, death, and insanity under his belt, he wasn't one to panic.

But he was days, maybe even hours, from becoming a father to a newborn again for the first time in thousands of years. He only wished his adopted Ramreel son, Rath, could be here to meet his new sibling. But Rath's herd had taken him on a pilgrimage to his ancestral Sheoulic home, and he wouldn't be back until next month.

His heavily pregnant wife, Cara, looked stunning in an aqua gown that floated around her ankles as she waddled -- her word, not his -- around the grounds of their mansion, greeting guests as they walked up the path from the Harrowgate. The party, an indoor/outdoor baby shower that Cara insisted wasn't a baby shower, was, so far, not out of control. But Wraith and Limos had just whipped up a batch of margaritas and tapped the kegs, so it wouldn't be long before the insanity started.

He wasn't sure he understood the baby shower not being a baby shower thing, but whatever Cara wanted, she got. And she'd wanted a party with all their friends and family to celebrate the pending arrival of their baby which, if all went according to plan, would be delivered next week by the same demon doctor who had delivered Thanatos's and Limos's kids.

I remember when demons were enemies.

It wasn't that long ago.

Hal, a young adult hellhound the size of a full-grown moose and so black it seemed to absorb the light surrounding it, ran past him to greet Cara, and although Ares was accustomed to his private island being overrun by the demonic canines, he still watched to make sure the thing didn't knock her over. It didn't, skidding to a halt in front of her, tail wagging, drool dripping from the corners of its gigantic maw.

She smiled and patted the beast on the muzzle, and it bounded away, happy to be acknowledged by the human his kind revered as a sacred healer.

The thunderous pound of footsteps alerted him to the approach of his two brothers, Thanatos and Reseph.

Thanatos, his sandy hair cut short save for the thin braid at each of his temples, clapped him on the back. Dressed casually in khakis and a black T-shirt that showed off some of the 3-D tattoos that had been layered on his skin by a demon tattoo artist, Than still maintained the deadly aura that surrounded him like a shroud.

"So, brother," he said. "Now that the day is almost here, have you decided what you're hoping for? A boy or a girl?"

Reseph snorted. "He's just hoping it's his."

"Funny, asshole." Ares punched his brother in the shoulder. His relationship with Reseph had been strained following Reseph's apocalyptic stint as Pestilence, but in the last couple of years things had warmed up enough that they could kid around again.

Laughing, Reseph took a swig of the foamy beer in his hand, and Ares cursed at the sight of the cup. Reseph always brought a bag of the damned things to every party, whether it was a formal ball for underworld royalty, or a casual beach volleyball game. Something about a country music song and the proper way to drink beer at a "shindig."

Ares wished he could blame Pestilence for Reseph's penchant for redneck party songs and disposable drinkware, but even Pestilence had better taste than Reseph.

"It was pretty amusing," Than said, raising his own beer to his lips. Beer in a floofing Red Solo Cup.

Ares ignored that and gestured to his beer. "Was that truly the only vessel you could find to drink from?"

"Sorry, forgot to bring one of the skulls of my enemies with me," Than said dryly. "So? You gonna answer the question? Boy or girl?"

"You tell me. You have one of each."

Thanatos's cruel lips turned up in a contented smile. His wife, Regan, had given their son a baby sister a few months ago, and Ares had never seen his brother happier. Which wouldn't be hard to do, given that the guy had suffered the most of any of them since the day they'd been cursed as Horsemen.

"You can't go wrong either way," Than said.

Probably not. But there were so many memories—good and bad—wrapped up with the memories of his sons that some small part of him hoped for a girl. A clean slate. A fresh start. But he'd love a son just as much, and maybe he could use the knowledge and experience he had now to make sure he didn't make the same mistakes he'd made with his first two sons.

Anxious to get the subject off of himself, Ares gestured to Reseph. "What about you? Are you and Jillian talking about kids?"

"Oh, floof, no."

Limos strode up, her bright purple sundress ruffling in the breeze, her flip flops slapping the stone pathway. "Why not? You love kids."

"I love *other people's* kids, and Jillian is right there with me." He shrugged. "For now, at least. It's not like we're not immortal and can't wait a century or two."

"True," Ares said roughly, his head still in the past. "But bad things happen in an instant."

"Time goes by quickly, brother," Thanatos said to Reseph. "In the blink of an eye an eon will have passed and Satan will be freed from prison."

"Whoa." Limos stepped into the middle of them all, arms outstretched. "This is a party. You know, to celebrate life. Stop with the doom and gloom. Why does this happen every time we're together?"

"My name is Death," Than said drolly.

"Mine is War," Ares reminded her.

Reseph raised his plastic floofing cup. "Pestilence."

"So, Famine," Ares said pointedly, "what was your question again?"

"Yeah, yeah." She looked over at Arik, who was introducing their daughter to Ares's warhorse, Battle. "At least tell me you picked a decent name for your kid. Something normal."

Normal was hard to define, especially for them, but he knew what she meant. Limos felt that they were, in most respects, living in a modern human world, so their children would benefit if they could blend in. Thanatos and Regan had agreed, choosing to name their kids Logan and Amber instead of, say, Doom and Gloom. Limos had opted for Keilani, a Hawaiian name associated with Heaven and royalty, and as the daughter of a Horseman and the granddaughter of a Radiant angel, the name fit.

"We can't narrow it down to less than two names for a girl and two names for a boy, and Cara is stubborn. This child may never be named."

"*Cara* is stubborn?" Limos looked around. "Where is she, anyway?"

"She said something about taking Lilliana some food."

Limos scowled. "What's up with that, anyway? I haven't seen Lilliana since that day I mentioned she looked like she was gaining weight."

Thanatos choked on his beer. "You did what?"

"Oh, chill. She didn't hear me. I just asked Cara if Lil was preggo. Never saw Lilliana again. Figured she was mad that I thought she was fat and started avoiding me." Her violet eyes shot wide. "That's why she went into hiding, isn't it? She is pregnant!"

Yes, that was why, but Ares had promised to keep it to himself, and he would.

"I haven't seen her either," Reseph said, and Thanatos concurred.

"That's because she's going to have the Grim Reaper's baby," Limos said, her violet eyes bright with the excitement of solving a puzzle. A potentially scandalous puzzle. "But wait, why would she be hiding out here instead of with her husband?"

"Let it go, Limos," Ares said. "No good will come of speculation."

"Yeah, well, when's the last time I let anything go?"

"Never," he muttered. "But listen to me. All of you. None of this 'speculation' can leave this island, and it had better not reach Azagoth's ears, or all of us will regret it."

According to Cara, Lilliana would leave before she herself gave birth, and frankly, Ares couldn't wait. Azagoth couldn't be happy about his wife residing with Ares and Cara, and no good ever came of Azagoth's cold anger.

"Speaking of Azagoth," Reseph said, "I heard he reopened the gates to Sheoul."

"Sort of." Thanatos waved to Logan, who was playing on the beach with Mace under Regan and Idess's watchful eyes. Ever faithful, Logan's pet hellhound, Cujo, gnawed on a Gargantua demon's knuckle bone a short distance away. "He only opened the gates to the *griminions* and those he trusts."

"How do you know?" Ares asked. Not even Lilliana had been able to contact Azagoth until this morning.

"Yesterday I sent Cujo in through the Inner Sanctum."

Smart. Ares couldn't believe he hadn't thought of that. Sheoul-gra might have been closed to everyone else, but hellhounds could still materialize inside the Inner Sanctum where the souls were kept, thanks to an ancient understanding between Hades and the hellhound king, Cerberus.

"And he delivered your message?" Ares asked.

Thanatos nodded. "But it turns out that he didn't need to. Azagoth had already prepared to reopen the gates today. No idea why."

"At breakfast this morning, Lilliana told us Azagoth saw a video that persuaded him to contact her. When he did, she convinced him to open the realm to souls and angels again."

"How?"

Ares's gaze flickered up to the balcony off Lilliana's suite. Cara was going to miss her. "She told him she wants to go home."

Limos clapped her hands in delight. "Because she's pregnant."

Ares just shook his head and gestured to the gathering around the appetizer and drink tables. "Why don't we join the party?" he said, jumping at any chance to get Limos off the topic.

But Limos was tenacious and not known to be able to keep juicy secrets.

Lilliana had best go home.

Soon.

Cara carried a tray laden with food and beverage into the closed wing of the mansion, locking the door behind her.

"Lilliana? Are you awake?"

"I'm in here," Lil called from the sitting room that looked out over the courtyard full of partygoers.

Cara entered and found Azagoth's mate curled up with a book near the window. "I brought you some appetizers from the party."

Lilliana's face lit up. "That's so thoughtful."

"I just wish you would reconsider joining us." Cara placed a glass and a pitcher of virgin sangria on the coffee table. "No one here will spill your secret."

Lilliana rested her hand on her swollen belly. "I can't take the risk. I just can't let anyone know I'm pregnant until I tell Azagoth first. It's not fair to him." She frowned. "And if he learns about the baby from someone else… yikes."

Cara set the tray down, thankful she wasn't in her friend's situation. They were both pregnant, having conceived within days of each other, but Lilliana, as an angel, had a slightly longer gestation period. And her husband was the Grim Reaper, a being known for his depth of evil and cruelty. Cara would *not* want to be mated to him. Although her own marriage to one of the Four Horsemen of the Apocalypse was probably looked on as equally terrifying by people who didn't know Ares.

And even some who did.

"He wouldn't…hurt you, would he?" Cara felt like a jerk asking that, but one never knew what went on behind closed doors, and she was feeling particularly protective of her friend.

Lilliana started. "No, of course not. Never. But he's got a reputation for killing the messenger. And he'd be very, very angry with me."

"But he understands why you left in the first place, right?" Cara plucked one of Suzanne's Caramel Pretzel Bites off the tray and popped it into her mouth, barely containing a moan. Suzanne had provided a lot of the food today, although she hadn't been able to stay for the party.

Lilliana nodded. "He does. And he's worked hard to learn to control his temper." She played eenie-meenie-miney-mo between a Bacon Wrapped

Stuffed Fig and a dish of Blueberry Lemon Angel Food Cake Trifle before settling on the fig. "It's time to go home."

The sea breeze blew through the open window, bringing with it laughter from the party below. "I don't mean to push you, but if the gates are open again, why haven't you gone?"

"I wanted to at least be here for the birth of your baby," Lilliana said, and as if her words were a signal, a dull but intense cramp wrapped around Cara's belly and climbed her spine like a ladder.

"Uh-oh."

Lilliana froze as she reached for the trifle. "What is it?"

The baby kicked, and Cara wondered if it had felt the cramp too. "I was planning to watch the beach volleyball game Reseph and Wraith are starting in a few minutes, and then I figured we'd open presents and serve cake afterward...but I think I might need to adjust the timetable." She hissed through what she was certain was a contraction. "I sort of had Shade jumpstart labor."

Lilliana jerked upright, trifle forgotten. "You did what?"

"I wanted this to be a baby shower. I wanted my entire family to be with us for the most important day of our lives. Besides, why not use the perks that come with having friends like the Sem brothers?" Cara reached behind her to massage the small of her back, but the ache was gone almost as quickly as it had come, a perk of being bonded with the hellhound race. Her pain was theirs, and through them, she healed with supernatural speed. "Don't worry. I cleared it with Eidolon a couple of weeks ago. He said it would be perfectly safe."

"And what did Ares have to say about that?"

Cara laughed. Ares had adapted to modern life -- mostly -- but his first, instinctive reaction to anything new was to revert to his primitive roots.

"He thought we should do the natural labor thing. Can you believe it? I mean, there's nothing natural about any of this." She rolled her eyes. "He got all ancient warrior, me man, you woman on me."

"I hear you." Lilliana gave a knowing laugh. Azagoth was even older than Ares. "And what did you say?"

"That it was my body, my rules." She smirked and popped a Goat Cheese Truffle into her mouth.

"And..." Lilliana prompted.

"And I told him that if he didn't like that, he could bite my ass."

One of Lilliana's delicate eyebrows arched in curiosity. "And what did he do?"

Cara smiled at the memory of his outrage, the way his face had turned as red as a Sora demon's butt. She hadn't known what he was going to do when he came at her like a tank, but she'd stood her ground, ready for anything.

"He bit my ass, we had sex, and he never brought it up again." She'd always loved the way Ares fought battles with her. They usually ended in bed. Another cramp tore through her, and she sucked in a harsh breath. "Maybe I should go find Eidolon." She cursed softly. "He might be a little pissed."

Coming to her feet far more smoothly than Cara could, Lilliana held out her hand to offer assistance. "I thought you cleared this with him."

"I did." She let Lilliana pull her to her feet. "He said it was fine but that I needed to tell him as soon as Shade did it. I forgot to find him after Shade did his thing."

Shade had warned her that labor could progress quickly, but she hadn't thought he meant practically instantly.

A sudden, screaming pain squeezed her abdomen and shot up her spine. "I'd better go." She gave Lilliana a hug, both chuckling at the physical awkwardness of a hug with two pregnant bellies.

"Congratulations," Lilliana murmured. "I'll see you and your little one soon."

Sooner, maybe, than expected, if the rush of liquid between Cara's legs was any indication.

It was finally time.

Ares's heart was in his throat as Cara sucked in a pained breath. They'd planned for the birth and had converted one of the guest rooms into a delivery room, but Ares hadn't planned on it being used this soon.

Obviously, Cara had different plans that no number of ass-bites had changed.

"Push, Cara," Eidolon said. "This should be the last one. Make it count."

"You got this," Gem, Eidolon's sister-in-law and a fellow doctor, had arrived with her mate, Kynan, just as Cara went into labor, and she'd volunteered to assist,

Gripping his hand so tightly his fingers went white, Cara bore down with a scream. He hadn't been present for his sons' births, and now he realized he had both missed out...and had been lucky. Seeing his mate in pain was torture he wished he could take upon himself.

An eternity later, Cara stopped screaming and flopped backward on the pillow. Two heartbeats passed, and then a baby's powerful cry rang out.

"Congratulations," Eidolon said as Gem clamped the cord. "Your little pony is a filly."

"A girl!" Ares shouted, his joyous shout making the art on the walls shake. "I have a daughter!"

Through the open windows, cheers and shouts of congratulations erupted from the party below. Outside the bedroom door, his siblings and their mates called out in celebration.

Gem wrapped the wailing baby in a warm towel and placed her in Cara's arms.

"She's so beautiful." His finger trembled as he brushed it over her delicate cheek. After thousands of years of witnessing and dealing death, he was finally a part of life. "But we still don't have a name for her."

The baby's cries grew quieter, turning to soft, contented mewls, but outside, the howls of a hundred hellhounds, maybe more, vibrated the entire island with their haunting song.

The door burst open, and the room filled with his siblings and their spouses. Reaver and Harvester remained below with the Sems and the rest of their friends, but they'd be up soon.

Thanatos and Reseph still had their damned plastic cups. "You hearing that?" Reseph stuck his head out the window. "What are they saying?"

Cara, her eyes wide with both exhaustion and amazement, looked up from the baby and smiled. "Aleka," she murmured. "That's what they're calling her."

"Aleka." Ares liked the sound of it on his tongue. "It's an ancient Greek name. It means protector. Defender of mankind." He could picture his daughter growing into both of those things. "It's a warrior's name."

Cara's gaze met his, and they both knew. "I think it sounds perfect," she said.

It *was* perfect. Everything about this day was perfect.

"To Aleka," Thanatos called out, but when everyone raised their drinks in celebration, Ares revised his thought.

Everything was perfect except those floofing red cups.

At Eidolon's okay and within an hour of giving birth, Cara had showered, dressed, and joined the party with her baby daughter. She wasn't even tired. The supernatural link she shared with every hellhound in existence allowed her to heal and replenish energy quickly, but she was still surprised that she felt this good.

Before joining up with everyone again, she'd taken Aleka to meet Hal, Cara's personal hellhound protector. Hal had given the infant a sniff and a gentle nudge of welcome, and then he'd poofed away to deliver Aleka's scent to the rest of the pack. Soon, all hellhounds would be able to identify her as one to be protected and never harmed.

Afterward, she'd gone to Lilliana to introduce her to Aleka...and to say goodbye. According to the terms of Lilliana's marriage to Azagoth, she wasn't supposed to leave Sheoul-gra except under very specific circumstances. Reaver had made it happen this time, but it wasn't as if Lilliana could come and go as she pleased. But they planned to keep in touch via whatever technology was available now and in the centuries to come.

And if, for any reason, Ares needed to speak to the Grim Reaper, Cara could use the opportunity to visit Lilliana.

Cara figured Ares would need to speak to Azagoth a lot more often in the future.

Now, with Reaver gone, escorting Lilliana to the one gate Azagoth had opened, Cara was surrounded by friends, family, and mountains of wrapping paper, boxes, and bags from the gifts she'd opened. The cake had been cut, a buffet had been put out, and while the kids played outside with an entire pack of hellhound babysitters, the alcohol flowed freely inside.

"Aleka seems to be loving Thanatos's cradle." Ares set a plate of food in front of Cara and bent over to admire their sleeping daughter.

"I can't believe how much time he spent carving it." She ran a finger along one ornately detailed railing, marveling at the scenes of battle and hellhound hunts etched in great detail on every surface. It wasn't exactly the ducks and bunnies she might have gone with, but she was living in a reality where her baby had also been given a dagger tempered with demon blood as a gift. So there was that. "It's incredible." She looked around the room at the pile of gifts. "Everything is incredible. We've surrounded ourselves with amazing people."

Ares straightened. "We have, haven't we?" He gestured to the two-foot tall clay jar wrapped with a bright red bow. "I mean, not everyone's relatives give them penises of unknown origin as a gift."

She laughed. "They're for the hellhounds, and Harvester and your father did give Aleka the most unique gift." The blanket, made in Heaven with the fleece of golden sheep, was guaranteed to quiet and comfort a fussy baby, and so far, the guarantee had held, with Aleka swaddled and sleeping peacefully.

"It's truly priceless." He sank down next to her. "And so are you." His gaze drifted back to Aleka as she kicked a tiny foot. "And so is she."

Cara pulled the plate of food over onto her lap. She hadn't had time to eat much today, and now that things had calmed down, she was starving. But as she reached for a pot sticker, she noticed Ares's faraway gaze.

"Hey, is everything okay?"

He didn't even have to ask what she was talking about. "Yes," he said, giving her a reassuring smile. "I loved my sons, and my guilt over their deaths will never fade, but now I can honor them by being a good father to their sister."

"You're going to be a great father." She used her foot to rock the cradle in a slow, easy rhythm. "Even though she's going to drive you crazy as a teenager."

Ares made a noise she'd never heard before. A noise that sounded suspiciously like panic. "Teenager?"

"Babies do grow into teenagers," she said in a teasing voice. "Takes approximately thirteen years." She envisioned life at that point in the future and grinned. "Imagine our family get-togethers in thirteen years. We think they're crazy now. Wait until the kids are all old enough to cause trouble."

The color drained from his face. "The Sem boys," he growled. "I swear, if one of them so much as looks at my daughter..."

She reached over and patted his hand. "Honey, they're all going to be looking at her." Cara gazed at the stunning little treasure in the cradle. "She's going to be amazing."

Friends and family started migrating over again with their plates of food, and Cara let herself be surrounded by the people who had become her world.

It was a world she'd entered reluctantly, but now she couldn't imagine it any other way.

Ares's story began in Sin Undone, the 5th book of the Demonica series, but it kicked off with a life of its own in Eternal Rider, the 1st book of the Lords of Deliverance series. See how the legends of the Apocalypse came to be! And if you're curious about how things end up for Lilliana, be sure to pick up CIPHER, available 04/09/19.

CELEBRATION FOOD AND SNACKS

Goat Cheese Truffles

1 cup pecans, pureed

1 cup dried cranberries

1 cup fresh parsley, chopped

1 cup grated Parmesan cheese

10 ounces goat cheese

4 ounces cream cheese

2 tablespoons honey

Place pecans, dried cranberries, fresh parsley and Parmesan cheese on 4 separate plates. In a large bowl, using a hand mixer, beat together the goat cheese, cream cheese and honey. Using a cookie scoop or melon baller, scoop out 12-15 rounds of cheese, roll into a ball, then roll in your desired topping (pecans, dried cranberries, fresh parsley, or Parmesan cheese. Place on a parchment lined cookie sheet and refrigerate for 1 hour before serving.

Seven Layer Greek Goddess

1 (8 ounce) container roasted garlic hummus

1 cup sour cream

1 cup fresh spinach

4 Roma tomatoes, chopped

1 cucumber, chopped

½ cup chopped red onion

½ cup crumbled feta cheese

½ cup Kalamata olives, chopped

Spread the hummus evenly across the bottom of a 9-inch pie or serving plate. Spread the sour cream over the hummus. Top with the spinach, then the tomatoes, cucumber, onion, feta cheese, and chopped Kalamata olives. Serve with pita chips.

Bacon Wrapped Stuffed Figs

4 ounces goat cheese

¼ teaspoon salt

¼ teaspoon pepper

24 fresh figs

12 slices bacon, cut in half

Preheat oven to 425 degrees. In a small bowl, combine goat cheese, salt and pepper. Slice each fig ¾ of the way down the center lengthwise. Fill with about a teaspoon of goat cheese then wrap with bacon. Secure with a toothpick and place on a parchment lined cookie sheet. Bake for 15-20 minutes or until bacon is crisp.

Mini Chicken Gyros with Easy Tzatziki

1 cup plain Greek yogurt

1 lemon, juiced

1 teaspoon salt

1 teaspoon pepper

1 teaspoon dried oregano

2 boneless, skinless chicken breasts

2 tablespoons oil

8 flour tortillas (soft taco size)

4 Roma tomatoes, sliced

½ red onion, thinly sliced

Tzatziki sauce

In a large bowl, combine the yogurt, lemon juice, salt, pepper and oregano. Add the chicken, cover and refrigerate for 24 hours. In a large non-stick skillet over medium heat, add the oil, remove the chicken from the marinade and place in the skillet. Cook on both sides for 5-7 minutes or until the internal temperature is 165 degrees. Remove from heat and cut into ½-inch strips. Place 2-3 strips on a flour tortilla. Top with tomatoes, onion and Easy Tzatziki.

Easy Tzatziki

1 cucumber, peeled

1 cup plain Greek yogurt

1 tablespoon minced garlic

1 tablespoon red wine vinegar

1 tablespoon fresh dill, minced

¼ teaspoon salt

¼ teaspoon pepper

Cut from the cucumber in half lengthwise. Scrape out seeds and grate cucumber. Place the grated cucumber in cheese cloth and squeeze out all excess liquid. In a medium bowl, add cucumber and remaining ingredients. Mix well, cover and refrigerate for 24 hours.

Pot Stickers

1 pound ground pork

½ cup chopped green onion

1 tablespoon minced garlic

1 tablespoon ground ginger

3 tablespoons soy sauce

1 teaspoon sesame oil

2 cups finely chopped cabbage

2 ½ cups flour

1 teaspoon salt

1 cup boiling water

2 tablespoons oil

In a large bowl, add pork, green onions, garlic, ginger, soy sauce, sesame oil and cabbage. Mix together, cover and refrigerate for 1 hour. Place flour and salt in a mixing bowl. Slowly pour in boiling water. Stir with a spoon until mixture forms a dough. Flour your hands and transfer dough to a work surface. Knead dough until it becomes smooth and elastic. Wrap dough ball in plastic, and let it rest about 30 minutes. Divide dough into 4 equal pieces. Cover 3 pieces with a dish cloth while you work the first piece. Roll dough into a small log about ¾ inches thick,

or the size of a thumb. Divide each log into 6 equal pieces. Roll each piece into a thin 3 ½-inch circle on a lightly floured surface to form the pot sticker wrappers. Repeat with the remaining dough pieces. Lightly moisten the edges of a wrapper with a wet finger. Place a small scoop of the ground pork mixture onto the center of the wrapper. Fold up the 2 sides and pinch together in the center. Pinch the remaining edges, forming "pleats" along one side. Tap the pot sticker on the work surface to slightly flatten the bottom; form a slight curve in it so that it stands upright in the pan. Repeat with remaining dough and filling. Heat oil in skillet over medium-high heat. Place about 6 or 7 pot stickers in the hot oil, flat side down. Cook until bottoms are golden brown, about 2 minutes. Pour in ¼ cup water and quickly cover the pan, then steam for 3 minutes. Uncover and reduce heat to medium. Continue cooking until water evaporates and bottoms are browned and crunchy, 1 or 2 minutes. Transfer to a warm serving dish. Repeat with remaining pot stickers.

Blueberry Lemon Angel Food Cake Trifle

1 (6 ounce) can frozen lemonade concentrate

2 (8 ounce) containers frozen whipped topping, thawed

1 (14 ounce) can sweetened condensed milk

1 prepared angel food cake, cubed

2 pints fresh blueberries

In a large bowl, using a hand mixer, combine the lemonade concentrate, 1 container whipped topping, and the sweetened condensed milk. In a trifle bowl, layer 1/3 angel food cake cubes, 1/3 lemon filling and 1/3 blueberries. Repeat twice more and top with 1 container whipped topping and additional blueberries.

Caramel Pretzel Bites

- 1 box brownie mix
- ½ cup milk chocolate chips
- ½ cup crushed pretzels
- ¼ cup water
- ⅔ cup oil
- 2 eggs
- Cream Cheese Icing (page 78)
- Pretzels for garnish
- Caramel Sauce

Preheat oven to 350 degrees. Line 24 mini muffin tins with liners. In a large bowl, combine the brownie mix, chocolate chips, crushed pretzels, water, oil and eggs together. Fill the muffin tins with batter and bake for 12-15 minutes or until a toothpick inserted in the center of a brownie comes out clean. Remove from oven and cool completely. Using a piping bag with a star tip, pipe on Cream Cheese Icing. Add a pretzel and top with Caramel Sauce.

Caramel Sauce

- 1 cup dark brown sugar
- ½ cup heavy cream
- 4 tablespoons butter
- ⅛ teaspoon salt
- 1 teaspoon vanilla extract

In a small saucepan over low heat, mix together all ingredients and continue to stir while cooking for 8-10 minutes. Remove from heat and allow to cool before serving.

AN INTERVIEW WITH
EIDOLON and TAYLA

When Dining With Demons
Spaghetti all'Angeliciana
Strawberries with Black Pepper Balsamic Sauce

Recipes from the Underworld
Beer Cheese Spread with Bite
Ghastbat (or Chicken) & Cheese Enchiladas with
Green Chile & Sour Cream Sauce
Orecchiette with Hell Weed (or Broccoli) and White Beans

For the Hell Pets
Cerby Snacks
Hellcat Bits
Hellhound Bites
Paw Balm

When you are dining with a demon you got to have a long spoon.
~ Navjot Singh Sidhu

AN INTERVIEW WITH EIDOLON AND TAYLA

It's freaking freezing in western Wisconsin when Eidolon and Tayla arrive at my house for dinner. My husband and son are at the movies, and the hellhounds, appropriately named Duvel (Dutch/Belgian dialect for "devil") and Hexe (German for "witch"), are in the backyard for the evening. Only the cat, Vegas (I know, right? Totally doesn't fit the theme, but she came with the name), is running around the house. She gives the newcomers a bored look before heading to the bedroom to get white fur all over my pillow. What grows on Vegas does not stay on Vegas.

I invite my guests inside. Tayla looks amazing with her burgundy hair piled high on her head in a messy, but classy twist, and Eidolon is as hot as ever in black slacks and a charcoal sweater that hides the *dermoire* on his right arm. The only glyphs visible are those on his hands and the mate-circle on his throat. Tayla has matching marks on her arm, transferred there when they bonded, but hers are also covered by her long-sleeved mustard blouse. I tell her I love the knee-high boots she's wearing over black leggings, and I'm just a little envious that she can walk on ice in three-inch heels.

The dogs are going insane at the back door, but they'll just have to stay there for a while.

"Don't worry," I say. "They'll settle down. Give them a Cerby snack they'll love you forever."

Eidolon cocks a dark eyebrow. "Cerby snack?"

"They're like Scooby snacks." I hang their coats in the closet. The new leather smell of Eidolon's jacket doesn't mask his natural, earthy scent Tayla is always going on about. She's right, though...someone should bottle that shit. "Except with a hellhound twist."

178

"Ah, Cerby, for Cerberus. Clever."

Yep, that's me. So clever that I can't even think of an appropriate response. But then, it's not every day that fictional characters come to life and hang with you for dinner, you know? And honestly, I'm a little in awe of them. Eidolon is a doctor who runs an infamous underworld hospital staffed by demons, vampires, and werewolves, and Tayla, despite being half demon, is a respected demon slayer who has saved countless lives.

I offer them drinks and appetizers, and then we settle down in the living room to chat. What follows is the official transcript from the evening.**

L: Tayla, I'm curious. How has your life changed since you and Eidolon mated and had a son?

She takes a sip of her wine. (It's called Naughty Girl, and it's fabulous and fitting.)

T: Sleep! Holy shit, I never get any sleep. It's a damned good thing my demon half doesn't need it.

I'm sure we all know that Soulshredders don't sleep. They hibernate for a year every two decades or so. As a half-breed, Tayla doesn't hibernate, but her need for sleep has been drastically reduced since Eidolon fused her demon DNA with her human DNA.

L: What keeps you busiest? Work? Motherhood? Maybe...Eidolon?

Tayla gives Eidolon a secret smile, and his mouth twitches in an arrogant smirk. It's obvious that he keeps her busy, and she doesn't mind losing sleep over it at all.

T: All of the above. I'm not complaining, though. I love my life. It's crazy, because I never even saw myself making it to thirty. Now I could live to be a few centuries old, and I'm a mother.

L: And how is little Sabre doing?

E: He's not so little anymore. He's in grade school now. *He grins proudly* Top of his class.

L: I wouldn't expect anything different.

T: He says he wants to be a doctor when he grows up. But last month he wanted to be a bus driver, so you never know.

No kidding. I wanted to be a veterinarian, an astronaut, a paleontologist, and a Battlestar Galactica pilot all by the time I was twelve.

L: When my son was little he wanted to be a soldier. Or a voice actor. Or a video game tester.

T: And what did he end up doing?

L: He got a degree in software engineering, so he may end up doing the video game thing eventually. Right now he's working for an IT company.

E: Sounds like he should take Stryke under his wing. My nephew is all about computers and technology.

The oven timer dings, telling me the garlic bread is ready, so we move to the table and I serve dinner. As we dish up the spaghetti all'angelicina, we get started with the reason they're here.

L: Are you ready for some reader questions?

Tayla's mouth is full, so she nods.

L: Okay, first one is for Eidolon. Michelle D. wants to know if you can share Wraith's phone number.

Eidolon barks out a laugh.

E: I'd post his number on Craig's List if he wasn't mated. But Serena would kick my ass. And probably hunt down and eat anyone who called him.

Understandably so. Sorry, Michelle, I tried.

L: Okay, next question, similar subject. My amazing assistant, Judie, wants to ask Tayla what it's like having Wraith for a brother-in-law.

Tayla doesn't hesitate.

T: It's like having an untrained pet.

E: That's a slight exaggeration.

Eidolon winds pasta around his fork.

E: He is potty trained.

T: True. But if you don't keep him busy with snacks he rips up your house.

I laugh, but I'm pretty sure she's serious. I let them eat for a minute and then hit them with another reader query from the sheet of paper next to my plate.

L: Madalyn S. is getting naughty with her question...she wants to know what dessert Tayla would like Eidolon to lick off her body after dinner.

Tayla's cheeks turn pink. It's sweet how the big, bad, demon slayer blushes.

T: Desserts he has licked off of me, or desserts we haven't yet tried?

I laugh again.

L: So dessert is popular in your house, I take it.

Eidolon's espresso eyes grow even darker as he takes in his mate.

E: I like a special dessert a couple of times a week.

T: Anything saucy is a favorite.

L: Then I have a fabulous dessert for you tonight. Saucy and spicy.

Tayla shivers in delight and I start to suspect that we will have an early night. They seem anxious to get home now. I throw out another reader question before they excuse themselves.

L: Kat D. wants to know if family life is what you thought it would be with each other and if you take vacations with your brothers and sisters.

T: I didn't have a family until I found Eidolon, so I didn't know what to expect. Turns out I love it and I wouldn't give it up for anything.

Eidolon graces us with a rare smile, barely noticeable through the wine glass he's drinking from. When he finishes drinking, he reaches for Tayla's hand.

E: I love my life and I can't imagine anything better. *he gives her hand a little squeeze* And yes, we do vacation with the extended family. Last month we went skiing with Sin and Con. Next month we're going with our brothers and their families to Disney World. And last week we went to a baby shower for Ares's mate, Cara.

L: I understand you delivered the baby.

E: Cara delivered the baby. I just caught it.

L: It's not like you to be modest.

T: He's not being modest. In this case, he's right. He was barely in time.

E: *curses* It wasn't my fault. If Shade hadn't helped things along—

T: Cara asked him to. *She reaches over and gives Eidolon a comforting pat on the arm.* It all turned out beautifully.

Eidolon agrees, and as I clear the table to serve dessert, I continue with the interview.

L: Okay, so Aliya A. has two questions. Eidolon, she wants to know if you worry about Sin having a child, given the complications that can arise due to her genetics. And Tayla, she asks if you secretly wish you could have a girl.

For those who don't know, Eidolon is a Seminus demon, a rare breed of incubi that only produces male offspring. His sister, Sin, is an anomaly. You can read about her and her twin brother in Ecstasy Unveiled and Sin Undone (Shameless plug).

E: *breaking into doctor mode and a smooth, deep voice that oozes professionalism and expertise* I'm not too concerned about Sin having a baby. She's tougher than Gargantua hide. She and Con aren't in any hurry to have children, so we'll deal with it when it happens. No matter what, she and her baby will have the best care on the planet.

Of that, I have no doubt. Maybe I can get him to look at that strange mole on my foot...

T: I've accepted that all of the children I give birth to will be boys, but I'd be perfectly happy to adopt a little girl of any species who needs a family.

Their eyes light up as I place dishes of strawberries with black pepper basalmic sauce in front of them.

L: *sitting with my own dish.* Emma J. asked an interesting question: If your siblings were cocktails, what would they be?

Eidolon, looking amused, eats a strawberry and appears to think on his answer. Finally, he nods.

E: Shade's a damned Moscow Mule, stubborn as shit. Wraith's a Snakebite. Lore...I'd say he's cheap rotgut in a dirty shot glass. *looks at Tay* What do think for Sin and Gem?

T: *looks at me* First of all, these strawberries are the bomb. I need the recipe before we leave.

Eidolon agrees, reaching over to wipe a bead of the sauce off her lower lip.

E: Remember that question about a dessert to lick off your body? *His voice goes velvet smooth, so seductive I feel like a voyeur* This is so floofing it.

L: Ahem. *I take a drink of ice water and fan myself* Yes, well, maybe we could get through a couple more questions before that happens?

T: *looking sheepish* Sorry. What was the question? Oh, yes, what kind of cocktail would Sin and Gem be if they were drinks. Sin is definitely a Sex on the Beach. Gem…she's an Ultra Violet.

I can't say I disagree with their choices.

E: Yeah, the Ultra Violet definitely fits. Gem just dyed her hair purple. She looks like a cartoon character.

T: She *is* a cartoon character. We all are. *turns to me* You know about the Demonica comic books, right? Someone is writing about our lives like it's fiction.

L: *Looking down at my dish of strawberries* Yeah, weird, huh?

E: *narrows his eyes at me* Do you know who the authors are?

L: Me? What? No.

Tayla and Eidolon look skeptical. I decide to change the subject. Quickly.

L: Hey, I have another question for you. This one's about Underworld General Hospital. I know it was constructed under the streets of Manhattan and that you've got a spell hiding it from human eyes, but Jackie M. wants to know if a human has ever accidentally stumbled upon it.

E: Not that I know of. It's possible, but anyone who has was probably devoured by the bloodwraiths stationed at the entrances.

I blink, my spoon paused at my mouth.

L: Are you serious?

E: *shrugs*

I don't remember there being any bloodwraiths in any of the books, but then, I can't remember what color eyes anyone has without looking it up, either. Except Thanatos and his yellow eyes and Limos with her violet ones. Oh, and Azagoth. Those emerald gems aren't easily forgotten. And Reaver! Sapphire blue is my favorite color. So, okay, I can remember a few things, but really, bloodwraiths? You'd think I'd remember that. But I'm not going to argue. Eidolon seems to be getting a little restless, so I want to get in a couple more questions before they have to leave.

L: Okay, we'll let that go and move on to a query from Frances M. She would like to know what it was like for Tayla to transition to demon cuisine, and Eidolon, how did you make it easier for her to give it a try?

E: *grimaces* I floofing hate demon food. Demons use the grossest shit. I was lucky my parents were mainly vegetarians.

L: Mainly?

Eidolon shoots me a withering stare that says he doesn't want to talk about it. That's cool. I know what Judicia demons eat during holidays, and I'd rather not ruin dessert, or my cookbook, with the details. Note for those who don't know: Seminus demons are parasitic. Remember how I said they're always male, Sin being the only exception? Well, these males impregnate females of other species, and those females give birth to purebred Seminus demons, so Eidolon grew up in a Judicia demon family with his biological mother.

T: You know, some demon food isn't terrible. I mean, a lot of demons who live in the human realm eat human food and cook with human ingredients. Sometimes they just change out the protein or they use special herbs found only in Sheoul, but really, some of it isn't bad.

E: And it's not like humans don't eat disgusting shit. Casu marzu? Hakarl? Pineapple on pizza?

I'll give him the wormy cheese and rotten shark meat, but come on! Pineapple is perfectly acceptable on pizza. As a professional, however, I put aside my personal feelings and continue with the interview.

L: Well, that was the perfect lead-in to my final question. Tayla, Brittney R. wanted me to ask you what you think is the most surprisingly delicious demon dish.

Tayla considers that for a moment.

T: Once there was a potluck thing at UGH, a Halloween party I think...

E: Yeah, we stopped doing that after someone cast a spell that made some of the decorations come to life.

T: I thought that was fun. I think this was the same party. Anyway, someone brought Ghastbat & Cheese Enchiladas. Ghastbat was actually pretty tasty.

Eidolon shoots her an 'are you kidding me' look.

E: You threw up.

T: That was after I found out there were fairy wings in the enchiladas.

Eew. It's going to be a while before I get that out of my head. Great question, Brittany!

So with that, we fell into conversations about food and travel, and then it was time for them to go. Saying goodbye was hard, but it always is. We fall in love with the people who come to life on the pages of books, and The End never comes easy. There have been times when I've even shed a tear or two.

Fortunately, the great thing about books is that we can revisit our friends whenever we want. They'll be there forever, sparking our imaginations and opening our minds, expanding our knowledge base, and bringing us comfort.

Romance novels especially speak to the core of who we are -- we're social creatures who want friends and mates. Every single one of us has experienced, or wants to experience, romance. It's something we all have in common. If you've dated, you've been a character in your own romance story.

So here's to romance and food. May your heart find what it's looking for, and if it finds it by way of the stomach, even better.

Cheers and love!

Eidolon and Tayla are the couple who started it all. You can read all about them in the first book of the Demonica series, *Pleasure Unbound*. And when I tell you it's a hot romance, I mean it. Don't say I didn't warn you...

**Not admissible as evidence in a carceris court

WHEN DINING WITH DEMONS

If you would like to try the dishes I made for the dinner with Tayla and Eidolon, I wrote them out for you. They're favorites in the Ione family, and they happen to be the same dishes Suzanne made for Declan in Her Guardian Angel, and for the record, he loved them. Because they're awesome, if I do say so myself...

Spaghetti all'Angeliciana (Sinful Version)

1 pound thick cut bacon, cut into 1-inch pieces*

2 tablespoons reserved bacon drippings*

2 cups raw spinach

1 (14 ounce) can whole or diced tomatoes
(fire-roasted provides a wonderful flavor)

4 shallots, chopped

1 clove garlic, minced

½ teaspoon - 1 teaspoon red pepper flakes (or to taste)

1 (28 ounce) can whole tomatoes

2 tablespoons butter*

1 pound Spaghetti*

Freshly grated Parmesan or Pecorino Romano for serving

Salt

Fresh basil leaves

Fry bacon until completely rendered and crispy, about 6-10 minutes. While bacon is cooking, pulse spinach and the small can of tomatoes a couple of times in a food processor or blender until mostly smooth.

When bacon is crisp, drain fat, reserving 2 tablespoons in the pan and turn heat to medium-low. Add the shallots, garlic, and red pepper flakes and cook, stirring, for 1 minute. Add large can of tomatoes and the blended tomato-spinach mixture and simmer, stirring occasionally, 30 minutes.

Meanwhile, fill a large pot with enough water to cook 1 pound of spaghetti. Bring to a boil. Add a generous amount of salt (make the water as salty as the ocean) and the pasta and cook according to package instructions for al dente.

Drain. Swirl 2 tablespoons butter into the sauce and toss with the spaghetti. Serve topped with freshly grated cheese. Garnish with fresh basil leaves.

*For Heavenly version:

Substitute olive oil for bacon drippings and butter

Substitute veggie or whole wheat pasta for traditional pasta

Substitute 4 ounces diced pancetta for bacon

Strawberries with Black Pepper Balsamic Sauce

¼ cup plus 2 teaspoons packed brown sugar or maple sugar

⅓ cup balsamic vinegar

½ teaspoon lemon juice

2 pounds fresh strawberries, hulled and quartered or sliced

½ teaspoon ground black pepper

Coarse ground pepper to taste

In a small saucepan, bring the 2 teaspoons of brown sugar, vinegar, and lemon juice to a simmer over medium-low heat and cook, stirring often, 3-4 minutes until thickened and reduced to about 3 tablespoons. Let cool.

In a large bowl, toss strawberries, ground pepper, and remaining brown sugar. Allow to rest at room temperature, stirring occasionally until the berries begin to release their juice, about 15 minutes.

Pour vinegar syrup into the berries, give a couple of grinds of fresh pepper, and toss gently to coat. Serve plain or with a dollop of sweetened mascarpone cheese.

RECIPES FROM THE UNDERWORLD

When putting together this book of recipes and stories, I realized my non-human friends and readers might feel left out if I didn't include recipes of some of their most popular dishes. In every episode of Angel in the Kitchen, Suzanne includes ways for the human dishes to be altered with Sheoulic ingredients, so I had her put together a menu of underworlder favorites that can be altered for human tastes, keeping in mind that humans and non-humans alike share this planet and therefore share many of the same ingredients; cinnamon is cinnamon in all the realms.

For the Snackers:

Beer Cheese Spread with Bite (2 ways)

2 (8 ounce) blocks cream cheese, softened

1 packet ranch dressing mix

8 tablespoons hoppy beer, preferably a very strong IPA

3 cups shredded sharp cheddar or beer cheddar

1-2 fresh demonfire peppers, seeded and chopped fine
(Humans: use jalapeños)

In a large bowl, beat the cream cheese on low speed until creamy, about 30 seconds. With the mixer on low, sprinkle in the ranch dressing mix, and then slowly add the beer. Mix until well blended, another 30 seconds or so. Fold in the shredded cheese and jalapeño or demonfire peppers. Wonderful with pretzels or pretzel chips.

Tip: This will set up in the refrigerator and be more like a spread. At room temperature it's more like a dip.

To serve hot:

Spread in a shallow dish and top with another cup of shredded cheese. Bake at 350 for 20-25 minutes, until bubbly and hot. Awesome with tortilla chips.

For the Carnivores:

Ghastbat (or Chicken) & Cheese Enchiladas with Green Chile & Sour Cream Sauce

2 cups cooked, shredded ghastbat (Humans: use chicken)

2 cups shredded Monterey Jack cheese, divided

2 (4 ounce) cans diced green chiles, divided

10 small flour tortillas

¼ cup chopped imp root (Humans: use green onions)

3 tablespoons butter

3 tablespoons flour

2 cups ghastbat bone broth (Humans: use chicken broth)

1 cup sour cream

Preheat oven to 350 degrees. Grease a 9 × 13-inch glass baking dish. Mix chicken/ghastbat, 1 cup cheese, and 1 can chiles. Roll up in tortillas and place in baking dish. Sprinkle with green onions/imp root. In a sauce pan, melt butter, whisk in flour and cook 1 minute. Gradually add broth and whisk until smooth. Heat over medium heat until thickened. Remove from heat and stir in sour cream and remaining chiles. Pour over enchiladas and top with remaining cheese. Bake 25 min covered. Remove foil and broil for 3-5 minutes until cheese is browned and bubbly.

For the Vegetarians:

Yes, contrary to popular belief, not all underworlders eat meat. Or people. Some, like the gentle Huldrefoxes, are vegetarians. This recipe is for our veggie-loving friends.

Orecchiette with Hell Weed (or broccoli) and White Beans

¼ cup extra-virgin olive oil

1 shallot, minced

8 bloodbath cloves, minced (Humans: use garlic)

1 teaspoon fresh fairy wings, minced (Humans: use oregano)

¼ teaspoon red pepper flakes (I use more!)

1 (15 ounce) can cannellini or great Northern beans

2 pounds hell weed, rinsed and cut into small florets (Humans: use broccoli)

12 ounces small shells or orecchiette

1 cup grated Parmesan or Asiago cheese

Salt and pepper

Put 4 quarts of water on the stove to bring to a boil. Heat oil in a 12-inch skillet over medium heat. Add shallot and cook about 2 minutes until softened. Add garlic/bloodbath cloves, oregano/fairy wings, and pepper flakes, and cook another 30 seconds. Stir in beans, cook 2 minutes, remove from heat and set aside.

To the boiling water, add broccoli/hell weed and 1 tablespoon of salt and cook, stirring occasionally, for 2 minutes. Use a slotted spoon to transfer broccoli/hell weed to the bean mixture.

Return water to boiling and add pasta. Cook according to package directions until al dente. Reserve 1 cup water, drain pasta, and return to pot. Add 1/3 cup of reserved water, the bean mixture, and cheese. Toss to combine. Salt and pepper to taste, adding more reserved water if needed.

For the Hell Pets

There was no way I could put my name on a cookbook that didn't have at least one recipe for the furry members of the family, because in my house, pets are family, and these are some of my favorite recipes. Hellhound and Hellcat tested and approved.

Cerby Snacks
(Get it? Like Scooby Snacks, but for Cerberus?)

1 cup cheddar cheese

1 cup whole wheat flour

1 tablespoon coconut oil or butter

⅓ cup milk

Combine first three ingredients and mix lightly. Gradually add milk until moistened – do not over stir. On lightly floured cutting board, knead mixture about 10 times. Roll out to about 1/4 inch thick and cut into 1-inch squares or use small cookie cutters.

Place on ungreased cookie sheet and bake at 350 for 10-15 minutes, until golden brown. Let cool completely. These are actually really tasty for humans too, especially sprinkled with a little salt before baking!

Hellcat Bits

1 egg white

1 (5 ounce) can tuna, salmon, or chicken, packed in water

½ teaspoon chopped fresh or dried catnip

In a small bowl, beat egg white until stiff peaks form. Scoop half of the beaten egg white into a food processor and add fish or chicken. Process until smooth. You really can't get it too smooth. Add mixture to remaining egg white and catnip. Fold gently until well mixed.

Use a pastry bag or spoon to drop in dime-sized dollops onto baking sheet lined with parchment paper. Bake at 325 for 25 minutes until dry and easily removed from the parchment. Dry on a cookie rack and store in an airtight container. May be refrigerated or frozen if not used within a week or two.

Hellhound Bites (Grain free treats)

I make these as "high value" treats for my hellhounds, and they love them! They're much more economical than store-bought treats, especially if you get the meat on sale.

1 pound lean beef - I like round steak, but I'll use anything on sale.
Garlic powder (optional)

Trim all excess fat. Sprinkle beef very lightly with garlic powder if desired. Cut into small cubes no larger than 1/2 inch square. Spread cubes on a cookie sheet so they aren't touching. Bake at 200 degrees, checking and turning every 1/2 hour. Bake until very dry and hard. Store in fridge.

Paw Balm

If you live in a cold climate, you have to protect those paws! This recipe is a must in our household. I have silicone paw molds that make nice little bars that are also perfect for gift giving. Simply warm in your hand for 30 seconds or so, and then rub the bar on your dog's paws. Also great for moisturizing their paws...and yours!

1 ounce beeswax (bar or beads)

4 tablespoons coconut oil

4 tablespoons olive or avocado oil

2 tablespoons shea butter

Few drops lavender oil (optional, but great for antibacterial properties and scent)

Melt the first 4 ingredients together in a small pan over low heat. When fully melted, remove from heat and add the lavender oil. Pour into a mold and allow to cool. Wrap tightly in plastic or in sandwich bags to store.

INDEX

APPETIZERS & SIDES

Bacon Wrapped Stuffed Figs 171

Beer Cheese Spread with Bite 191

French Onion Soup 153

Fried Mac and Cheese Bites 152

Goat Cheese Truffles 169

Grilled Oysters with Spicy Butter 74

Loaded Grits in a Bacon Cup 39

Mini Chicken Gyros with Easy Tzatziki 172

Pot Stickers 173

Salsa with a Vengeance 109

Seafood Platter 125

   -Beer Battered Fries 127

   -Buttermilk Hush Hellhound Puppies 126

   -Fried Catfish 126

   -Fried Shrimp 125

Seven Layer Greek Goddess 170

Steak Bruschetta with Onion Jam 79

PASTRIES & SALADS

Angel Food Cake French Toast 38

Pumpkin Spice Loaf with Spiced Icing 42

MAIN DISHES

Bloody Mary Pie	40
Breakfast Burrito	45
Caprese Chicken with Balsamic Glaze	81
Cauliflower Pizza	124
Chicken Biscuit Pot Pie	149
Chicken Parmesan	122
Egg in a Hell Hole Avocado Toast	43
Ghastbat (or Chicken) & Cheese Enchiladas with Green Chile & Sour Cream Sauce	192
Grilled Beef Skewers with Wasabi Aioli	105
Gumbo	107
Maple Sausage and Waffle Casserole	44
Meatloaf and Monster Mash Cupcakes	121
Orecchiette with Hell Weed (or broccoli) and White Beans	193
Seafood Linguini	75
Soft Shell Crab BLT	154
Spaghetti all'Angeliciana	187
Spicy Sheoul Shrimp	37
Spicy Sticky Ribs	110
Stuffed Flank Steak	76
Taco Spaghetti	151
White Chicken Chili	106
Zesty Lemon Mahi Mahi	108

DESSERTS

Bananas Foster Crème Brulee 80
Blueberry Lemon Angel Food Cake Trifle 175
Caramel Pretzel Bites 176
Cherry Hand Pies 150
Dark Chocolate Chipotle Brownies 104
Hell Frozen Over Smoothie Pops 120
Red Devil's Food Cake 77
Strawberries with Black Pepper Balsamic Sauce 189

DRINKS

Hair of the Hellhound 36

For the Hell Pets

Cerby Snacks 195
Hellcat Bits 196
Hellhound Bites 197
Paw Balm 198

OTHER BOOKS BY LARISSA IONE

DEMONICA/LORDS OF DELIVERANCE SERIES

Pleasure Unbound (Book 1)

Desire Unchained (Book 2)

Passion Unleashed (Book 3)

Ecstasy Unveiled (Book 4)

Eternity Embraced ebook (Book 4.5) (NOVELLA)

Sin Undone August (Book 5)

Eternal Rider (Book 6)

Supernatural Anthology (Book 6.5) (NOVELLA)

Immortal Rider (Book 7)

Lethal Rider (Book 8)

Rogue Rider (Book 9)

Reaver (Book 10)

Azagoth (Book 11)

Revenant (Book 12)

Hades (Book 13)

Base Instincts (Book 13.5)

Z (Book 14)

Razr (Book 15)

Hawkyn (Book 16)

Her Guardian Angel (Book 17)

MOONBOUND CLAN VAMPIRES SERIES

Bound By Night (book 1)

Chained By Night (book 2)

Blood Red Kiss Anthology (book 2.5)

OTHER BOOKS BY SUZANNE MCCOLLUM JOHNSON

Southern Bits & Bites

Southern Kid Bits & Mom Bites

Southern Bits & Bites: Our 150 Favorite Recipes

Writing with Lexi Blake

Master Bits & Mercenary Bites

Master Bits & Mercenary Bites~Girls Night

Writing with J. Kenner

Bar Bites: A Man of the Month Cookbook

Writing with Kristen Proby

Indulge With Me: A With Me in Seattle Celebration